The president's triumphal progress continued late into the night

FROM THE EARTH
TO THE MOON

By JULES VERNE

Translated by

JACQUELINE and ROBERT BALDICK

*With colour plates
and line drawings in the text by*

W. F. PHILLIPPS

LONDON: J. M. DENT & SONS LTD
NEW YORK: E. P. DUTTON & CO. INC.

JULES VERNE, who may well be described as the inventor of science fiction, was born at Nantes in France on 8th February 1828 and died at Amiens on 24th March 1905.

After studying law for a while in Paris, he began to write for the theatre, achieving some success with comedies and librettos for comic operas. But some travel stories which he wrote for a magazine showed him where his true gifts lay, and he contributed 'Five Weeks in a Balloon' to a new periodical for young readers, Hetzel's 'Magazine d'Éducation', in 1862. It was issued in book form the following year, and became the first of Verne's long series of 'Extraordinary Voyages'—tall tales of travel based so firmly on scientific and geographic fact, and introducing such convincing and attractively recognizable characters, that they seem not only possible but probable.

Verne's second book, 'A Journey to the Centre of the Earth' (1864), still remains a fantasy, but the next one, 'From the Earth to the Moon' (1865), with its continuation 'Around the Moon' (1870) has become fact.

In the same year as 'Around the Moon' Verne produced his most famous book 'Twenty Thousand Leagues Under the Sea', the thrilling story of a voyage by the submarine 'Nautilus' commanded by the mysterious Captain Nemo, written a quarter of a century before underwater travel was actually achieved.

'Around the World in Eighty Days'—a record trip in 1873—is the most famous of the many other extraordinary voyages Verne related next. Captain Nemo reappeared in one of the best of all shipwreck stories, 'The Mysterious Island' (1875), and many more strange experiences were described in more than fifty other narratives, from 'The Floating City' (1871) and 'Hector Servadac, or Life on a Comet' (1877) to 'The Master of the World' (1904) and 'The Barsac Mission', published posthumously.

From 1870 all Verne's works were issued in numerous English translations, and have been as popular on this side of the Channel as in their native France. The best of them are as fresh and as exciting today as when they were written a hundred years ago —even where Verne's daring prophecies have become commonplace of the machine age. For, as Marshal Lyautey said early this century, 'the advances made by the human race are merely the realization in life of what was fiction in the novels of Jules Verne'.

R. L. G.

First published in this edition 1970

© Illustrations, J. M. Dent & Sons Ltd, 1970. © English translation, J. M. Dent & Sons Ltd and E. P. Dutton & Co. Inc., 1970. All rights reserved. No part of this publication may be reproduced, stored in a retrieval system, or transmitted, in any form or by any means, electronic, mechanical, photocopying, recording or otherwise, without the prior permission of J. M. Dent & Sons Ltd. Made in Great Britain at the Aldine Press, Letchworth, Herts, for J. M. Dent & Sons Ltd, Aldine House, Bedford St, London.

ISBN: 0 460 05088 5

CONTENTS

CONTENTS

ILLUSTRATIONS

COLOUR

BLACK AND WHITE

Introduction

'IF WISHES were horses, beggars would ride'—and if they were space-rockets, the Moon would have been visited more than two thousand years ago. Although the poets of ancient Greece were still writing of the Moon-goddess Selenē driving across the sky in her silver chariot and landing on Mount Latmos in Asia Minor to visit Endymion in his eternal sleep, the scientists of the day knew perfectly well that a visitor to the Moon would find himself in another world.

Thus Anaxagoras about 450 B.C. described the Moon as 'an incandescent solid, having in it plains, mountains and ravines', and Philolaus at the end of the same century was suggesting that 'the Moon has an earthy appearance because, like our Earth, it is inhabited throughout by animals and plants'.

The Greeks were not quite sure of its distance or its size— 'larger than the Peloponnese', according to Anaxagoras—and they did not doubt that the atmosphere extended all the way, as was, indeed, still believed by scientists only a century and a half ago.

It would be difficult to get there, but not impossible; and what it was like no one could possibly tell until the journey had actually been made. So the satirist Lucian in the second century A.D. was able to write perhaps the first account ever penned of a fictional trip to the Moon, sending his hero Icaro-Mennipus flying on his way with an eagle's wing strapped to his right arm and a vulture's to his left.

It was not Lucian's aim to describe the world of the Moon in this satire, for Icaro-Mennipus was really on his way to Heaven to visit Zeus and the other gods of Olympus. But in his *True Story*—in which, he says: 'There is but one thing I can be sure is absolutely true—namely, that it is one long lie from start to finish!'—his ship is blown up to the Moon on a waterspout (rather like the 'twister' in *The Wizard of Oz*), and his adventures there are even more fantastic than those of Baron Munchausen sixteen hundred years later.

Lucian was writing fantasy, but the first Lunar Voyage in English was, according to the scientific knowledge of its period, as accurate science fiction as anything written by Ray Bradbury or Brian Aldiss. This was *The Man in the Moone* by Francis Godwin, Bishop of Hereford, first published in 1638, though probably written some years earlier.

His hero, Domingo Gonsales, went to the Moon by mistake. Being wrecked on the island of St Helena, then uninhabited, he constructed a 'flying chariot' which he trained the wild swans or *ganzas* to draw through the air. But when the time came for them to migrate, they proceeded to do so while harnessed to the chariot in which Gonsales was sitting. The naturalists of the period were of the opinion that wild birds migrated to the Moon in winter—so up went the *ganzas* taking Gonsales with them, and arriving after eleven days' swift flying.

The possibility of an actual trip to the Moon was considered seriously by another Bishop, this time of Chester, John Wilkins, who published in 1638 (without knowing anything about Godwin's book until several years later) *A Discovery of a New World, or a Discourse Tending to prove that 'tis Probable there may be another Habitable World in the Moon. With a Discourse Concerning the Probability of a Passage thither.*

'I do seriously, and upon good Grounds, affirm it possible to make a Flying Chariot,' Bishop Wilkins maintained. 'So that notwithstanding all the seeming impossibilities, 'tis likely enough, that there may be means invented of Journeying to the Moon. And how happy shall they be that are first successful in this attempt!'

It was to be 340 years before these happy men were to make the first successful landing on the Moon, and meanwhile other works of fiction appeared which tackled the problem of getting there with greater or less scientific forethought.

One writer of satire, the French wit and duellist Cyrano de Bergerac toyed with rocket-propulsion among other less probable methods without realizing that he held the true key to space-flight.

His first attempt, though scientific in 1657, sounds more like Wonderland science to us now. Knowing that the Sun drew up the dew from the grass each morning he collected it one night in a sufficient number of bottles which he fastened to a belt round his waist. Sure enough, when the Sun rose it drew up the dew as usual, and as the dew could not escape from the bottles they went up with it—and as they could not escape from Cyrano's belt, he was drawn up as well. However, he found that he had miscalculated the speed, and that the Moon would not come between him and the Sun at the right moment. So, to avoid being drawn into the Sun, he began breaking bottles, and landed safely—in Canada, the Earth having turned under him, and so having made the first trip across the Atlantic by air.

In Canada he proceeded to build a flying-machine with revolving wings. But on his first attempt it went wrong and crashed in the market square of Quebec. Being much bruised, Cyrano left his machine where it was and went off to annoint himself all over with beef-marrow.

When he returned he found that the soldiers of the garrison had fastened rockets all round the back of his 'chariot', meaning to launch it as a fiery dragon to frighten the Red Indians. In his anxiety to save his machine Cyrano leapt into it and tried to take off the rockets. But he was too late: off they went and up went the chariot.

Not all the way, however, for the rockets gave out and the machine fell back to earth. But Cyrano continued on his course, for superstition, if not science, at the time assured him that the Moon draws up the marrow of animals—and he, be it remembered, was plentifully smeared with beef-marrow!

There were several flights of fancy in the eighteenth century, but the next to be based on sound scientific knowledge was *The Unparalleled Adventure of one Hans Pfaall*, published in 1835, by Edgar Allan Poe—who is thus as much the ancestor of science fiction as he is of the detective story and the quest for hidden treasure.

Hans went up in a balloon: for it was still believed that the atmosphere continued all the way to the Moon. It was assumed, however, that much of it was so thin that a man could not breathe for a good part of the journey, so Hans took with him a supply of oxygen and a kind of oxygen tent. He set his balloon speeding in the right direction by means of a gigantic explosion of gun-powder which produced a rush of hot air, and on the seventeenth day of his voyage came within the gravitational pull of the Moon: the balloon turned over, and he descended safely onto the surface of the satellite three days later.

The next trip, that described in the present book, is by far the most famous in fiction, and reads like a dress-rehearsal for the real thing. In fact, an account of it written by an expert in technical terms might easily deceive:

'The true inaugural manned Moon flight must be accredited to Professor Impey Barbicane, president in 1865 of the Gun Club of Baltimore, Maryland, U.S.A. It was he who led the preparations for this first mission, which was undertaken by himself and fellow-astronauts Ardan and Nicoll—preceded by an experimental launch of a smaller sub-orbital spacecraft with an animal "crew".

'Blast-off for the manned attempt took place at 10.47 p.m. on 30 November 1865, when the giant Columbiad launcher dispatched the spacecraft from the concrete pad at Stone Hill, Tampa, Florida, its sonic booms echoing across the five-million-strong crowd that had gathered to watch the astronauts' departure.

'Their spacecraft was a cylindro-conical aluminium vehicle 12 feet long, 9 feet in diameter and weighing 12,230 pounds. It left the Earth's atmosphere at 24,545 m.p.h. and, on nearing the Moon, fired its retro-rockets to bring it into an orbit that eventually descended to within 30 miles of the lunar surface. After completing several lunar orbits, it made a successful return journey to Earth, splashing down in the Pacific Ocean at 1.17 a.m. on 12 December 1865, some 250 miles off the west coast of America, where the occupants were picked up by the U.S.S. *Susquehanna*.'

Compare this with an account written by the same expert of the first actual trip round the Moon:

'At nine minutes before 8 a.m. on 21 December 1968, three American space travellers named Borman, Anders and Lovell left the Earth, from Cape Kennedy in southern Florida. Their spacecraft, Apollo 8, was a cylindro-conical metal vehicle, of which the inhabited part was 12 feet long and 13 feet in diameter, with a weight of 12,392 pounds. It left the Earth's atmosphere travelling at 24,227 m.p.h., and, a little less than three days later went into orbit round the Moon, descending to 69 miles above the lunar surface. After completing ten lunar orbits, it made a successful return journey to Earth, splashing down in the Pacific Ocean at 10.51 a.m. on 27 December 1968 about 1,000 miles south-west of Hawaii, where the occupants were picked up by the U.S.S. *Yorktown*.'

Jules Verne (1828–1905) has been described as the true inventor of the submarine, the luxury liner and the aeroplane: *From the Earth to the Moon* and *Around the Moon* prove that he has also a secure place in the history of space flight—certainly as a prophet with an uncanny gift of scientific foresight.

He was also a superb story-teller, whose tales do not seem to lose any of their freshness even after a hundred years. He has but to bid us follow him and he will lead us absorbed for twenty thousand leagues under the sea, around the world in eighty days, on a journey into the interior of the earth—or, at this very moment, if you let him, on an amazing trip From the Earth to the Moon!

Roger Lancelyn Green.

I

The Gun Club

DURING the Civil War in the United States an influential club was founded in the city of Baltimore, Maryland. It is well known how rapidly the military instinct developed in that nation of shipowners, merchants and mechanics. Shopkeepers jumped their counters to become captains, colonels and generals without having gone through the military academy of West Point: yet they soon rivalled their colleagues of the Old World in the 'art of war' and, like them, won victories by means of a lavish expenditure of ammunition, money and men.

But the sphere in which the Americans far surpassed the Europeans was the science of ballistics. Not that their guns reached a higher degree of perfection, but they were of unusual dimensions, and consequently attained hitherto unheard-of ranges. When it comes to grazing fire, plunging fire, or direct fire, oblique fire, enfilading fire or harassing fire, the English, French and Prussians have nothing to learn; but their cannons, howitzers and mortars are just pocket pistols compared with the awe-inspiring engines of the American artillery.

This fact should surprise no one. The Yankees, the best mechanics in the world, are engineers in the way the Italians are musicians and the Germans metaphysicians—by birth. Nothing could be more natural, therefore, than for them to apply their bold ingenuity to the science of ballistics. The wonders achieved in this domain by men like Parrot, Dahlgren and Rodman are known to everyone. Armstrong,

Palliser and Treuille de Beaulieu could bow to their transatlantic rivals.

So during the terrible struggle between the North and the
South the artillerymen reigned supreme; the Union newspapers
enthusiastically praised their inventions, and there was no
tradesman so humble, no idler so naïve that he did not rack
his brains day and night calculating fantastic trajectories.

Now when an American has an idea, he looks for another
American to share it. If there are three of them, they elect a
president and two vice-presidents. If there are four, they appoint
a secretary, and the office is ready for work. If there are five,
they convene a general meeting, and the club is fully con-
stituted. That was what happened in Baltimore. A man who
invented a new cannon associated himself with the man who
cast it and the man who bored it. They formed the nucleus of
the Gun Club. A month after its formation it numbered 1,833
full members and 30,575 corresponding members.

One strict condition was imposed on every candidate for
membership: he had to have invented or at least improved a
cannon; or, in default of a cannon, a firearm of some description. It must, however, be admitted that the inventors of
fifteen-shot revolvers, pivoting carbines or sabre pistols were
not held in high regard. The artillerymen invariably took
precedence over them.

'The esteem in which they are held,' one of the most learned
orators of the Gun Club said one day, 'is proportional to the
mass of their guns, and in direct ratio to the square of the
distances attained by their projectiles.'

This was very nearly an application of Newton's law of
gravity to the sphere of psychology.

Once the Gun Club had been founded it is easy to imagine
the results achieved in this field by the inventive genius of the
Americans.

Their engines of war attained colossal proportions, and their
projectiles went beyond all bounds to cut inoffensive bystanders
in half. All these inventions left the timid instruments of
European artillery far behind, as the following figures reveal.

In the 'good old days' a 36-pound cannon-ball fired from the flank at a distance of 100 yards would go through thirty-six horses and sixty-eight men. The art of gunnery was then in its infancy. Since then it has come a long way. The Rodman cannon, which fired a cannon-ball weighing half a ton a distance of seven miles, could easily have felled 150 horses and 300 men. The Gun Club actually considered testing the accuracy of this calculation, but while horses were willing to take part in the experiment, it unfortunately proved impossible to find any human volunteers.

Be that as it may, these guns had a murderous effect, and at every shot combatants fell like corn under the scythe. Compared to such projectiles, what was the famous cannon-ball which put twenty-five men out of action at Coutras in 1587, or that other which killed forty infantrymen at Zorndorf in 1758, or that Austrian cannon which felled seventy enemy soldiers with every shot at Kesseldorf, in 1742? What were those amazing barrages at Jena or Austerlitz which decided the outcome of the battle? Now in the Civil War there had been some *real* gunfire! At the Battle of Gettysburg a conical projectile fired from a rifled cannon struck down 173 Confederates, and during the crossing of the Potomac a Rodman cannon-ball sent 215 Southerners into an obviously better world. Mention must also be made of a formidable mortar invented by J. T. Maston, the distinguished member and perpetual secretary of the Gun Club, which proved even more lethal, for when it was first fired it killed 337 people—admittedly by exploding!

What can we add to these figures, so eloquent in themselves? Nothing. The reader will therefore find it easy to accept the following calculation made by the statistician Pitcairn. By dividing the number of the Gun Club's victims by the number of members, he found that each member had killed an average of 2,375 and a fraction men.

Consideration of such a figure makes it clear that the sole aim of that learned society was the destruction of the human race for philanthropic reasons, and the improvement of weapons of war, regarded as instruments of civilization. The

Gun Club was an assembly of Exterminating Angels, who at the same time were thoroughly decent chaps.

It must be added that these fearless Yankees did not confine themselves to theory, but risked their lives in battle. They included officers of all ranks, from lieutenants to generals, and soldiers of every age, from those who had just begun their military career to those who had grown old over their gun-carriages. Many of those whose names were inscribed in the Gun Club's book of honour fell on the battlefield, and most of those who returned bore the marks of their indisputable courage. Crutches, wooden legs, artificial arms, steel hooks, indiarubber jaws, silver craniums, platinum noses—nothing was missing from the collection ; and the aforementioned Pitcairn calculated that among the members of the Gun Club there was not quite one arm between four men, and only one leg between three.

But these valiant artillerymen took no notice of these trifles, and they felt justifiably proud when the reports of a battle gave the number of casualties as ten times the number of projectiles fired.

One day, however, one sad and sorry day, peace was signed between the survivors of the war. The sound of gunfire gradually died down, the mortars fell silent, the howitzers were muzzled for years to come, the cannons went back with bowed heads to the arsenals, the cannon-balls were piled up in the parks, the memories of bloodshed faded, the cotton-plants grew luxuriantly in the richly fertilized fields, the garments of mourning wore thin like grief itself and the Gun Club remained sunk in tedious inactivity.

True, a few gluttons for work still devoted their energies to ballistic calculations and went on dreaming of gigantic shells and incomparable projectiles. But what was the use of evolving theories which could never be put into practice? Consequently the club rooms became deserted, the servants dozed in the ante-chambers, the newspapers gathered dust on the tables, sounds of sad snoring came from dark corners, and the members of the Gun Club, once so noisy, but now reduced to silence by a disastrous peace, gave themselves up to daydreams of platonic artillery.

'This is terrible,' the worthy Tom Hunter said one evening while his wooden legs were charring in the fireplace of the smoking-room. 'There's nothing to do, nothing to hope for! What a tedious existence! Where are the days when we were awakened every morning by the joyful boom of the cannon?'

'*Where are the days when we were awakened every morning by the joyful boom of the cannon?*'

'Those days are gone,' replied the dashing Bilsby, trying to stretch his missing arms. 'How wonderful they were! You could invent a howitzer and try it out on the enemy as soon as it was cast. Then you came back to camp with a word of praise from Sherman or a handshake from McClellan! But now the generals have become shopkeepers again, and instead of cannon-

B

balls they're firing off inoffensive cotton-bales. The future looks bleak for artillery in America!'

'You're right, Bilsby, it's a cruel disappointment,' exclaimed Colonel Blomsberry. 'One day you give up your quiet life, you learn how to use a gun, you leave Baltimore and go off to war, you fight heroically, and then, two or three years later, you have to lose the fruit of all your efforts and sink into idleness with your hands in your pockets.'

Whatever he might say, the valiant colonel would have been hard put to it to demonstrate his own idleness in this way, though not from lack of pockets.

'And not a war in sight!' said the famous J. T. Maston, scratching his gutta-percha cranium with his iron hook. 'There's not a cloud on the horizon, and that when there's so much to to be done in the science of artillery! Only this morning I drew up a working drawing, with plan, section and elevation, of a mortar that's destined to change the laws of war!'

'Really?' said Tom Hunter, involuntarily recalling Maston's last invention.

'Yes,' replied Maston. 'But what was the use of making all those calculations and conquering all those difficulties? I was just wasting my time. The New World seems to have made up its mind to live in peace; and our bellicose *Tribune* has got to the point of predicting approaching catastrophes arising out of this scandalous increase of population.'

'All the same, Maston,' replied Colonel Blomsberry, 'they are still fighting in Europe in support of the nationalist principle.'

'What of it?'

'Well, there might be something for us to do over there; and if they accepted our services . . .'

'What an idea!' cried Bilsby. 'Working on ballistics for a lot of foreigners!'

'That would be better than doing no ballistic work at all,' retorted the colonel.

'Quite so,' said J. T. Maston; 'but it's out of the question.'

'Why?' asked the colonel.

'Because their ideas of promotion in the Old World are

contrary to all our American habits. Those people think a man can't become a general unless he's served as a second lieutenant first, which is like saying you can't aim a gun properly unless you've cast it yourself!'

'Ridiculous!' said Tom Hunter, stabbing the arms of his easy chair with his Bowie knife. 'If that's how things are, there's nothing left for us to do but plant tobacco and distil whale-oil.'

'What!' roared J. T. Maston. 'Are you suggesting that we shan't spend the rest of our lives improving firearms? That there'll be no new opportunities to test the range of our projectiles? That the sky will never again be lit up by the flash of our guns? That no international difficulties will arise to enable us to declare war on some transatlantic power? That the French will never sink a single one of our steamers, and that the English won't hang a few of our countrymen in defiance of the laws of humanity?'

'No such luck, Maston,' replied Colonel Blomsberry. 'Not one of those things will happen and, even if it did, we wouldn't take advantage of it. Americans' susceptibility is on the decline and we're turning into a nation of women!'

'Yes, we're humiliating ourselves!' said Bilsby.

'And we're being humiliated!' said Tom Hunter.

'That's all too true,' J. T. Maston said with fresh vehemence. 'There are hundreds of reasons for fighting, and yet we don't fight! We save on the arms and legs of people who don't know what to do with them! Why, without going out of our way to find a reason for going to war, didn't America once belong to the English?'

'Undoubtedly,' replied Tom Hunter, furiously poking the fire with the end of his crutch.

'Well then,' said J. T. Maston, 'why shouldn't England in turn belong to the Americans?'

'That would be only fair,' said Colonel Blomsberry.

'Go and suggest that to the President of the United States,' cried J. T. Maston, 'and you'll see what sort of reception he'll give you.'

'It won't be a very pleasant reception,' Bilsby muttered between the four teeth he had saved from battle.

'By heaven,' cried J. T. Maston, 'he won't get my vote at the next election!'

'Nor mine!' all the bellicose cripples shouted together.

'In the meantime,' J. T. Maston went on, 'if I'm not given an opportunity to try out my mortar on a real battlefield, I'll resign from the Gun Club and go and bury myself in the wilds of Arkansas.'

'And we'll go with you,' replied the others.

Things had reached this pass, with everyone getting more excited and the club threatened with approaching dissolution, when an unexpected event occurred to prevent such a deplorable catastrophe.

The day after this conversation every member of the club received a circular in the following terms:

Baltimore, 3 October

The President of the Gun Club has the honour to inform his fellow members that at the meeting of the 5th instant he will make an announcement which is likely to be of the greatest interest to them. He accordingly urges them to suspend all other business and attend the above meeting in accordance with the present invitation.

Impey Barbicane,
President of the Gun Club

2

President Barbicane's announcement

On 5th October, at eight o'clock in the evening, a dense crowd filled the rooms of the Gun Club at 21 Union Square. All the members of the club who lived in Baltimore had responded to their president's invitation. As for the corresponding members, express trains were bringing them into the city in hundreds. Large though the main hall was, it was totally inadequate to accommodate this crowd of learned members, and so they overflowed into the adjoining rooms, the corridors and even the courtyard outside. There they encountered the common herd who were crowding around the doors, each one trying to push his way to the front, all eager to discover the nature of President Barbicane's important announcement, pushing, jostling and squeezing one another with that freedom of action peculiar to a populace raised in the idea of self-government.

That evening a stranger who had happened to find himself in Baltimore would have been unable to gain admission to the main hall for love or money. That was reserved exclusively for the resident or corresponding members of the club; nobody else was allowed into it, and the local notabilities and municipal councillors were obliged to mingle with the ordinary citizens if they wished to catch word of what was happening inside.

In the meantime the main hall presented a curious sight. This vast room was wonderfully suited to its purpose. Lofty pillars formed of superposed guns resting on bases made of massive mortars supported the delicate arches, which looked like cast-iron lacework. Trophies consisting of matchlocks, blunderbusses, arquebuses, carbines and every other sort of firearm, ancient and modern, were picturesquely interlaced across the walls. Gas jets blazed from a thousand revolvers grouped together to form chandeliers, and this splendid lighting was completed by clusters of pistols and candelabra made up of bundles of rifles. Models of cannons, bronze castings, targets riddled with holes, metal plates battered by the Gun Club's cannon-balls, assortments of rammers and sponges, strings of shells—in short, all the apparatus of the artilleryman— astonished the eye by their surprising arrangement and gave the impression that their real purpose was more decorative than deadly.

In the place of honour, protected by a magnificent glass case, was a piece of a breech, broken and twisted by an explosion— a precious relic of J. T. Maston's mortar.

At the far end of the hall the president, flanked by four secretaries, occupied a large platform. His chair, resting on a sculptured gun-carriage, was shaped to represent a thirty-two inch mortar. It was pointed at an angle of ninety degrees and suspended from trunnions, so that the president could swing in it as in a rocking-chair, a pleasant convenience in hot weather. On the desk, a huge plate supported by six carronades, stood an inkpot of exquisite elegance, made of a beautifully chased bullet, and a bell which could be made to emit a report like a revolver shot. During heated arguments this novel kind of bell was only just loud enough to be heard above the voices of this legion of excited artillerymen.

In front of the desk, benches arranged in zigzags, like the trenches in a fortified position, formed a series of bastions and curtains reserved for the members of the Gun Club; and that particular evening it could be truly said that the ramparts were fully manned. The members knew the president well enough to be sure that he would not have summoned them without a very good reason.

Impey Barbicane was a calm, cold, austere man of forty, with an eminently serious and concentrated mind; punctual as a chronometer, with an imperturbable temperament and an unshakeable character; adventurous if not chivalrous, yet bringing practical ideas to bear on even his most daring enterprises; a typical New Englander, a colonizing northerner, a descendant of those Roundheads who proved so baneful to the Stuarts, and an implacable enemy of the gentlemen of the South, those Cavaliers of his motherland. In short, he was a Yankee through and through.

Barbicane had made a large fortune in the lumber business. Put in charge of the artillery during the war, he showed himself to be fertile in new ideas. With his bold conceptions he made a notable contribution to the development of artillery warfare, and gave a remarkable impetus to experimental research.

He was a man of average height and, by a rare exception in the Gun Club, had all his limbs intact. His strongly marked features seemed to have been drawn with a square and a scriber; and if it is true that, to judge a man's character one must look at him in profile, Barbicane, seen from the side, revealed unmistakable signs of energy, boldness and sang-froid.

At the moment he was sitting motionless and silent in his armchair, deep in thought, turned in upon himself, sheltered beneath his top hat, one of those black silk cylinders which seem to be screwed onto all American skulls.

His fellow members were chatting loudly around him, but without distracting him. They were questioning one another, venturing suppositions, scrutinizing their president and trying in vain to solve the mystery of his imperturbable face.

When the thunderous clock of the great hall struck eight, Barbicane suddenly rose to his feet as if he had been worked by a spring. Silence fell over the hall, and the speaker began in somewhat grandiloquent tones:

'Gentlemen, it is already too long since a sterile peace plunged the members of the Gun Club into deplorable inactivity. After a period of some years which was full of incident we had to abandon our work and stop short on the road of progress. I do not hesitate to say openly that any war

. . . he was sitting motionless and silent . . . sheltered beneath his top hat . . .

which would put our weapons back in our hands would be welcome. . . .'

'Yes, war!' cried the impetuous J. T. Maston.

'Hear, hear!' came shouts from all over the hall.

'But war,' Barbicane continued, 'is impossible in the present circumstances; and despite the hopes of my honourable interrupter, more long years will go by before our guns thunder again on a battlefield. We must resign ourselves to this fact and look for some other outlet for our consuming energy!'

The members sensed that their president was approaching the crux of his speech, and gave him all their attention.

'For a few months, gentlemen,' Barbicane went on, 'I have been wondering whether, while confining ourselves to our speciality, we could not undertake some great experiment worthy of the nineteenth century, and whether the progress which has been made in ballistics might not enable us to bring it to a successful conclusion. I have accordingly reflected, worked and calculated; and my studies have resulted in a conviction that we must bring off a project which would appear impractical to any other country. This project, which I have worked out with great care, is the subject of my address to you tonight. It is worthy of you; it is worthy of the Gun Club's past; and it cannot fail to make a great noise in the world.'

'A great noise?' cried an ardent artilleryman.

'A great noise in the true sense of the word,' replied Barbicane.

'Don't interrupt!' said several voices.

'I therefore beg you, gentlemen,' the president went on, 'to give me your full attention.'

A thrill of excitement ran through the audience. After rapidly fixing his hat more firmly on his head, Barbicane continued his speech in a calm voice:

'There is not one of you, gentlemen, who has not seen the moon, or at the very least heard of it. Do not be surprised that I should talk to you about the Queen of the Night, for it may be our fate to be the Columbuses of that unknown world. Try to understand my plans, help me to the best of your ability, and I will lead you in conquering the moon. And its name will join those of the thirty-six states which form this great Union.'

'Hurrah for the moon!' the Gun Club shouted with one voice.

'The moon has been the object of much study,' Barbicane went on. 'Its mass, density, weight, volume, composition, movements, distance and role in the solar system have been precisely determined. Charts have been drawn of its surface with a precision which equals or even surpasses that of the maps of the earth. Photography has given us pictures of our satellite of incomparable beauty. In short, we know everything about the moon that the mathematical sciences, astronomy, geology and optics can teach us about it. But until now no direct communication has been established with it.'

A violent stir of interest and surprise greeted this remark of the speaker.

'Allow me,' he continued, 'to remind you in a few words how certain ardent spirits, setting off on imaginary journeys, have claimed to have discovered the secrets of our satellite. In the seventeenth century a certain David Fabricius boasted of having seen some inhabitants of the moon with his own eyes. In 1649 a Frenchman, Jean Baudoin, published a *Journey to the World of the Moon by Domingo Gonzales, Spanish Adventurer*. At about the same time Cyrano de Bergerac brought out that famous story of a lunar expedition which obtained so much success in France. Later on, Fontenelle, another Frenchman— the French have always been very interested in the moon— wrote *The Plurality of Worlds*, a masterpiece in its day, but the march of science crushes even masterpieces underfoot! About 1835 a pamphlet translated from the *New York American* appeared in France which told how Sir John Herschel, having been sent to the Cape of Good Hope to carry out some astronomical studies there, had brought the moon to an apparent distance of eighty yards, by means of a telescope equipped with internal lighting. He was reported to have clearly seen caves occupied by hippopotami, green mountains fringed with gold lacework, sheep with ivory horns, white deer and inhabitants with membraned wings like those of bats. This pamphlet, the work of an American called Locke, obtained an enormous success, but it was soon revealed to be a scientific hoax, and the French were the first to laugh at it.

'Laugh at something written by an American!' cried J. T. Maston. 'Why, that's grounds for going to war!'

'Not so fast, my good fellow. Before laughing at it, the French had been completely taken in by our compatriot's work. To bring this rapid historical sketch to an end I will only add that a certain Hans Pfaal of Rotterdam, setting off in a balloon filled with gas extracted from nitrogen and thirty-seven times lighter than hydrogen, reached the moon after a journey lasting nineteen days. This journey, like the others I have mentioned, was purely imaginary, but it was the work of a strange, contemplative genius who was also a popular American writer. I refer to Edgar Allan Poe!'

'Hurrah for Poe!' shouted the audience, electrified by the president's words.

'So much,' Barbicane went on, 'for those purely literary efforts, which were totally incapable of establishing serious relations with the Queen of the Night. However, I must add that a few practical spirits have made serious attempts to enter into communications with the moon. Thus, a few years ago, a German geometrician proposed sending a scientific commission to the Siberian steppes. There, on those vast plains, by means of reflectors, the members of the commission would draw huge geometric figures, including the square of the hypotenuse. "Any intelligent being," said the geometrician, "is bound to understand the scientific purpose of that figure. The inhabitants of the moon, if they exist, will reply with a similar figure, and once communication has been established, it will be a simple matter to create an alphabet which will enable us to converse with them." So said the German geometrician, but his proposal was never put into practice, and so far no direct link has ever been established between the earth and its satellite. It has been left to the practical genius of the American people to make communication with the sidereal world. The means of doing this are simple, easy, certain and infallible, and they are the subject of the proposal I am about to put forward.'

These words were greeted by a hubbub, a storm of exclamations. There was not a single member of the audience who was not captivated, uplifted, carried away by what the speaker had just said.

'Hear, hear!' they shouted all over the hall.

When the excitement had subsided, Barbicane resumed his interrupted speech in a more solemn voice.

'You are aware,' he said, 'of the progress made in ballistics in recent years, and to what degree of perfection firearms would have attained if the war had continued. You are also aware that the strength of cannons and the expansive power of gunpowder are to all intents and purposes unlimited. Well, starting from that principle, I asked myself whether, using a sufficiently large cannon, constructed to ensure the required degree of resistance, it might not be possible to send a projectile to the moon.'

A gasp of amazement escaped from a thousand panting breasts; then there was a moment's silence like that profound stillness which precedes a thunderstorm. And sure enough, a thunderstorm did burst forth, but it was a thunder of applause, shouts and cries which made the whole hall tremble. The president tried to speak, but all in vain. It was a good ten minutes before he managed to make himself heard.

'Let me finish,' he continued coldly. 'I have studied the question from every angle and tackled it boldly, and from my incontrovertible calculations I have reached the conclusion that a projectile endowed with an initial velocity of 36,000 feet per second, and aimed at the moon, is bound to reach it. I therefore have the honour, gentlemen, to suggest to you that we undertake that little experiment!'

3

Effect of Barbicane's announcement

Iᴛ ɪs impossible to describe the effect produced by the president's last words. What cries! What yells! What a succession of shouts of 'Hurrah!' and 'Hip, hip, hurray!' and all the other enthusiastic noises in which the American language is so rich! The uproar and confusion were indescribable. Mouths shouted, hands clapped, feet pounded the floor of every room. If all the weapons in that artillery museum had been fired at once, they would not have caused a greater commotion among the sound waves. There is nothing surprising about that. There are gunners who are almost as noisy as their guns.

Barbicane remained calm in the midst of this enthusiastic clamour. Perhaps he wanted to say a few more words to his fellow members, for his gestures demanded silence, and his explosive bell was worn out with repeated detonations. Nobody so much as heard it. Soon he was torn from his seat, carried aloft in triumph, and passed from the hands of his loyal comrades into the arms of a no less excited crowd.

Nothing can ever astonish an American. The French have often asserted that the word *impossible* is not in their language, but they have obviously been talking about the wrong language. In America everything is easy, everything is simple and, as for mechanical difficulties, they are solved before they arise. No true Yankee would ever have allowed himself to see so much as the semblance of a difficulty between Barbicane's plan and its realization. For the Americans, a thing is no sooner said than done.

The president's triumphal progress continued late into the night. It was a real torchlight procession. Irishmen, Germans, Frenchmen, Scotsmen and all the other heterogeneous individuals who make up the population of Maryland gave voice in their native tongues; and the hurrahs, cheers and bravos mingled together in an indescribable din.

As for the moon itself, as if realizing that it was the object of all this commotion, it was shining with serene magnificence, eclipsing the surrounding stars with its intense radiance. The Americans all looked up at its sparkling disk. Some of them waved to it, others called it pet names; some sized it up with their eyes, others shook their fists at it. Between eight o'clock and midnight an optician on Jones Fall Street made a fortune selling telescopes. The Queen of the Night was ogled like a great lady. The Americans treated it with a proprietorial arrogance, as if fair Phoebe belonged to those bold conquerors and were already part of the territory of the Union. And yet they were only planning to send a projectile to the moon—a rather brutal way of establishing relations, even with a satellite, but very common among civilized nations.

Midnight came and went, and the enthusiasm of the crowds showed no sign of waning. It was maintained at an equal level in all classes of the population; judges, scientists, business men, shopkeepers, stevedores, intelligent people and greenhorns all felt stirred to their very depths. This was to be a national enterprise; so every part of the city, the quays washed by the waters of the Patapsco, and the ships imprisoned in their docks, were overflowing with crowds of people drunk with joy, gin and whisky. Everybody was conversing, perorating, discussing, arguing, approving and applauding, from the gentlemen taking their ease on the bar-room sofas with mugs of sherry cobbler [1] to the watermen getting drunk on knock-me-downs [2] in the gloomy taverns of Fell's Point.

[1] A mixture of rum, orange juice, sugar, cinnamon and nutmeg. This yellowish beverage is drunk out of a mug through a glass straw.

[2] A terrifying drink of the lower classes.

However, about two o'clock in the morning the general excitement subsided. President Barbicane succeeded in getting home, worn out, shattered and exhausted. Hercules himself could not have stood up to such enthusiasm. The crowds gradually left the streets and squares. The four railways from Ohio, Susquehanna, Philadelphia and Washington, which meet in Baltimore, scattered the multitude to the four corners of the United States, and the city returned to a condition of comparative calm.

It would be a mistake to think that Baltimore was the only city which fell a prey to such excitement on that memorable evening. The great cities of the Union—New York, Boston, Albany, Washington, Richmond, New Orleans, Charleston, Mobile—from Texas to Massachusetts and from Michigan to Florida, all shared in the same delirium. The thirty thousand corresponding members of the Gun Club had all seen their president's letter, and they had been waiting with equal impatience for the famous announcement of 5th October. The result was that same evening, as fast as the words came from the speaker's lips, they were transmitted all over the Union on telegraph wires at a speed of 248,447 miles per second. It can therefore be said with absolute certainty that at one and the same moment the United States of America, a country ten times as big as France, shouted a single 'Hurrah!', and that twenty-five million hearts, bursting with pride, beat with the same pulse.

The next day fifteen hundred daily, weekly, fortnightly and monthly newspapers and journals took up the matter. They examined it under all its various aspects—physical, meteorological, economic or moral—and from the point of view of its influence on civilization and the political situation. They wondered whether the moon was a finite world, or whether it was capable of undergoing some further transformation. Was it like the earth before its atmosphere existed? What did the face of the moon which was hidden from the earth look like? Although sending a projectile to the moon was all that had been suggested so far, every paper saw this as a starting point for a whole series of experiments. They all hoped that one day America would penetrate the last secrets of that mysterious orb, and some even seemed to fear that its conquest might seriously affect the balance of power in Europe.

Once the project had been discussed not a single journal expressed any doubt that it would be brought to a successful conclusion. Reviews, pamphlets, bulletins and magazines published by scientific, literary and religious societies all drew attention to its advantages; and the Natural History Society of Boston, the American Society of Science and Art of Albany, the Geographical and Statistical Society of New York, the American Philosophical Society of Philadelphia and the Smithsonian Institution of Washington sent countless letters of congratulations to the Gun Club, together with offers of immediate assistance and money.

Thus it can be said that no other proposal ever attracted so much support; hesitations, doubts, anxieties were out of the question. As for the jokes, caricatures and songs which would have greeted the idea of sending a projectile to the moon in Europe, and particularly in France, they would have been very dangerous to anyone composing them in America; all the 'life-preservers' [1] in the world would have been powerless to save him from the general indignation. There are some things one simply doesn't laugh at in the New World.

So from that day on, Impey Barbicane became one of the greatest citizens of the United States, something like the Washington of science. One incident among many will show the extent to which a whole people became suddenly devoted to a single man.

A few days after the memorable meeting of the Gun Club the manager of an English theatrical company announced that he was going to put on *Much Ado About Nothing* at the Baltimore theatre. The population of the city, seeing the title as an insulting reference to President Barbicane's project, invaded the theatre, broke up the benches and forced the unfortunate

---

[1] A pocket weapon made of flexible whalebone and a metal ball.

manager to change his programme. Having a good sense of humour, he bowed to the public will and replaced the offending comedy with *As You Like It*; and for several weeks his company played to packed houses.

4

Reply from the Cambridge Observatory

IN THE meantime, in the midst of all the praise being heaped upon him, Barbicane did not waste a single moment. The first thing he did was to gather his fellow members together in the offices of the Gun Club. There, after some discussion, they agreed to consult some astronomers on the astronomical part of the enterprise; once their reply had been received they could then discuss the mechanical means, and nothing would be neglected in order to ensure the success of this great experiment.

A letter in very precise terms containing some specific questions was accordingly sent to the observatory at Cambridge, Massachusetts. That city, where the first university in the United States was founded, is justly famous for its observatory. There scientists of the highest merit are to be found assembled; there the powerful telescope is to be seen which enabled Bond to resolve the nebula of Andromeda, and Clarke to discover the satellite of Sirius. The trust which the Gun Club placed in that famous institution was justified in every way.

Two days later, the impatiently awaited reply was delivered to President Barbicane.

It read as follows:

The Director of the Cambridge Observatory
to the President of the Gun Club in Baltimore.

Cambridge, 7 October

Dear Mr President,

On receipt of your letter of the 6th inst., addressed to the Cambridge Observatory on behalf of the members of the

22

Baltimore Gun Club, our staff met at once and prepared the following reply:

The questions you put to the Observatory staff were these:
1. Is it possible to send a projectile to the moon?
2. What is the precise distance between the earth and its satellite?
3. If a-projectile is given sufficient initial velocity, how long will it be in transit, and consequently when must it be fired in order to strike the moon at a given point?
4. At what precise moment will the moon be in the most favourable position to be reached by the projectile?
5. At what point in the sky must the cannon firing the projectile be aimed?
6. What position in the sky will the moon occupy at the moment the projectile is fired?

Regarding the first question: Is it possible to send a projectile to the moon?

Yes, it is possible, provided the projectile is given an initial velocity of 36,000 feet per second. Our calculations show that that velocity is sufficient. As one moves away from the earth, the force of gravity diminishes in inverse ratio to the square of the distance; in other words, at three times a given distance, the force of gravity is nine times weaker. Consequently the weight of the projectile will rapidly decrease, and will finally be reduced to zero at the moment when the attraction of the moon exactly balances the attraction of the earth, that is to say when $\frac{47}{52}$ of the journey has been completed. At that moment the projectile will cease to have any weight, and if it passes that point it will travel onwards to the moon by the sole effect of lunar attraction. The theoretical possibility of the experiment is therefore established beyond question; as for its successful accomplishment, that depends solely on the power of the cannon employed.

Regarding the second question: What is the precise distance between the earth and its satellite?

The moon does not describe a circle round the earth, but an ellipse, of which our globe occupies one of the foci. It follows that the moon is nearer to the earth at some times than at others, or, in astronomical terminology, sometimes at apogee and sometimes in perigee. Now the difference between the two distances is too great to be ignored. At apogee the moon is 247,552 miles from the earth, and in perigee only 218,657 miles away, making a difference of 28,895 miles, or more than one-ninth of the total distance. Calculations must therefore be based on the distance to the moon in perigee.

Regarding the third question: If a projectile is given sufficient initial velocity, how long will it be in transit, and consequently when must it be fired in order to strike the moon at a given point?

If the projectile were to maintain its initial velocity of 36,000 feet per second indefinitely, it would take only about nine hours to reach its destination; but that velocity will be constantly decreasing, and our calculations show that the projectile will take 300,000 seconds, or eighty-three hours and twenty minutes, to reach the point where the attractions of earth and moon are evenly balanced. From that point it will fall onto the moon in 50,000 seconds, or thirteen hours, fifty-three minutes and twenty seconds. It should therefore be fired ninety-seven hours, thirteen minutes and twenty seconds before the moon arrives at the point aimed at.

Regarding the fourth question: At what precise moment will the moon be in the most favourable position to be reached by the projectile?

In accordance with what has been said above, it is first of all necessary to choose the period when the moon is in perigee, and also the moment when it is at the zenith.[1] This will further reduce the distance by the length of the earth's radius, i.e. 3,919 miles, so that the actual distance to be covered will be 214,976 miles. But while the moon reaches

---

[1] The zenith is the point in the sky directly above the observer.

perigee every month, it is not always at the zenith at that
precise moment. It is only at long intervals that those two
conditions coincide, and it would be best to wait for such a
moment. Now, by a fortunate chance, on 4th December next
year the moon will fulfil both conditions: at midnight it will
be in perigee, i.e. at its shortest distance from the earth, and
at the same time will reach the zenith.

Regarding the fifth question: At what point in the sky
must the cannon firing the projectile be aimed?

On the basis of the foregoing observations, the cannon must
be aimed at the zenith. Its line of fire will thus be perpendicular to the plane of the horizon, and the projectile will
escape more rapidly from the earth's attraction. But for the
moon to reach the zenith of a given place, the latitude of
that place must not be greater than the moon's delineation,
in other words, the place must be somewhere between the
equator and the twenty-eighth parallel, north or south.[1] In
any other place the line of fire would have to be oblique, and
that would militate against the success of the experiment.

Regarding the sixth question: What position in the sky
will the moon occupy at the moment the projectile is fired?

At the moment the projectile is fired into space, the moon,
which travels thirteen degrees, ten minutes and thirty-five
seconds every day, will have to be four times that quantity
from the zenith, i.e. fifty-two degrees, forty-two minutes and
twenty seconds, a figure which corresponds to the distance
it will travel during the flight of the projectile. But as the
deviation which the rotation of the earth will impart to the
projectile must also be taken into account, and as the projectile will only reach the moon after a deviation equal to
sixteen times the radius of the earth, or about eleven degrees

[1] It is in fact only between the equator and the twenty-eighth parallel
that the moon reaches the zenith at its culmination. Beyond the twenty-
eighth parallel, the moon is farther away from the zenith the closer one
approaches the pole.

of the moon's orbit, these eleven degrees must be added to those representing the moon's journey mentioned above, making a total, in round figures, of sixty-four degrees. Thus at the moment of firing the line of sight to the moon will be at an angle of sixty-four degrees from the vertical.

These are the answers to the questions put to the Cambridge Observatory by the members of the Gun Club.

To sum up:

1. The cannon must be installed in a region situated between the equator and the twenty-eighth parallel, north or south.
2. It must be aimed at the zenith.
3. The projectile must be given an initial velocity of 36,000 feet per second.
4. It must be fired on 1st December next year, at thirteen minutes, twenty seconds before eleven o'clock at night.
5. It will strike the moon four days after its discharge, at precisely midnight on 4th December, just as the moon reaches the zenith.

The members of the Gun Club must therefore begin at once the preparations necessitated by an enterprise of this sort and be ready to fire the projectile at the time we have indicated, for if they miss this date of 4th December they will not find the moon in the same conditions of perigee and zenith for another eighteen years and eleven days.

The staff of the Cambridge Observatory place themselves entirely at the Gun Club's disposal with regard to all questions of theoretical astronomy, and hereby add their good wishes to those of all other Americans.

For the staff of the Cambridge Observatory:

J. M. BELFAST
Director

5

The romance of the moon

An observer endowed with infinitely penetrating powers of sight, and placed at that unknown centre around which the world gravitates, would have seen myriads of atoms filling space during the chaotic period of the universe. But little by little, as the centuries went by, a change took place; a law of attraction became apparent, which the hitherto wandering atoms obeyed; these atoms joined together chemically, according to their affinities, formed themselves into molecules and made up those nebulous masses with which the depths of space are scattered.

These masses were promptly animated by a rotary movement around their central point. This centre, made up of indeterminate molecules, began spinning around and progressively condensing. Moreover, in accordance with the immutable laws of mechanics, as its volume decreased through condensation its rotary movement accelerated, and, since these two effects continued, there resulted a principal star, the centre of the nebulous mass.

If he had looked closely the observer would then have seen the other molecules in the mass behaving like the central star, condensing in the same way in a progressively accelerating rotary motion, and gravitating around it in the form of countless stars. A nebula, one of five thousand, according to the astronomers' latest count, had been formed.

Among these five thousand nebulae there is one that men

have called the Milky Way. It contains eighteen million stars, each of which has become the centre of a solar system.

If the observer had specially examined one of the smallest [1] and dullest of those eighteen million stars, the fourth-class star we proudly call the sun, all the phenomena which gave rise to the formation of the sun would have taken place before his very eyes.

He would in fact have seen the sun, still in a gaseous state and composed of mobile molecules, turning on its axis to complete its process of concentration. This movement, faithfully obeying the laws of mechanics, would have accelerated as the sun's volume diminished, and a time would have come when centrifugal force would have triumphed over centripetal force, which tends to push molecules towards the centre.

Then another phenomenon would have taken place before the observer's eyes, as the molecules situated in the plane of the equator, flying off like a stone from a sling whose cord has suddenly snapped, would have gone and formed a series of concentric rings round the sun, like those of Saturn. In their turn these rings of cosmic matter, caught up in a rotary movement around the central mass, would have broken up and disintegrated into secondary nebulosities, in other words into planets.

If the observer had then fixed his attention on these planets he would have seen them behaving exactly like the sun and giving birth to one or more cosmic rings, composed of those minor stars we call satellites.

Thus, going from the atom to the molecule, from the molecule to the nebulous mass, from the nebulous mass to the nebula, from the nebula to the principal star, from the principal star to the sun, from the sun to the planet and from the planet to the satellite, we have the whole series of changes undergone by the heavenly bodies since the beginning of the world.

The sun seems lost in the vast spaces of the stellar universe,

[1] According to Wollaston, the diameter of Sirius must be twelve times that of the sun, or over ten million miles.

yet according to the latest scientific theories it is part of the
nebula we know as the Milky Way. However small it may seem
in the midst of the ethereal regions, it is the centre of a system
and really enormous, for it is 1,400,000 times bigger than the
earth. Around it gravitate eight planets which came from its
very entrails at the beginning of creation. These, going from
the closest to the most distant, are Mercury, Venus, the earth,
Mars, Jupiter, Saturn, Uranus and Neptune. In addition,
moving in regular orbits between Mars and Jupiter, there are
some other smaller bodies, possibly the wandering debris of a
star broken into several thousand pieces, ninety-seven of which
have so far been discovered by the telescope.[1]

Some of these attendants which the sun maintains in their
elliptical orbits by means of the great law of gravity have
satellites of their own. Uranus and Saturn have eight each,
Jupiter has four, Neptune may have three and the earth has
one. This last satellite, one of the smallest in the solar system,
is called the moon, and it was the moon which the Americans
had boldly decided to conquer.

Because of its comparative proximity, and the rapidly
changing spectacle of its various phases, the Queen of the Night
originally shared mankind's attention with the sun. But the sun
is tiring to look at, and the splendour of its light forces human
observers to lower their eyes.

Pale Phoebe, more humane in comparison, complaisantly
allows herself to be seen in all her modest charm; she is gentle
on the eye and very unassuming, yet she sometimes takes the
liberty of eclipsing her brother, radiant Apollo, without ever
being eclipsed by him. Realizing what a debt of gratitude they
owed this faithful friend of the earth, the Mohammedans
calculated their months on the basis of her revolutions.[2]

The nations of antiquity devoted a special cult to that chaste
goddess. The Egyptians called her Isis; the Phoenicians knew

[1] Some of these asteroids are so small that a man could run all the way
round them in the space of a single day.

[2] Each revolution takes about twenty-nine and a half days.

her as Astarte; the Greeks worshipped her under the name of Phoebe, daughter of Leto and Zeus, and they explained her eclipses by Diana's mysterious visits to the handsome Endymion. Legend has it that the Nemean lion roamed the deserts of the moon before appearing on earth, and the poet Agesianax, quoted by Plutarch, celebrated in his verses those gentle eyes, that charming nose and those kindly lips formed by the bright parts of the adorable Selene.

But while the ancients understood very well the character, temperament and moral qualities of the moon from the mythological point of view, even the most learned among them were extremely ignorant of its geography.

Several astronomers of ancient times, however, discovered certain peculiarities of the moon which have now been confirmed by science. While the Arcadians claimed to have lived on the earth at a time before the moon existed, while Tatius regarded it as a fragment broken off the sun, while Aristotle's disciple Clearchus described it as a polished mirror in which images of the ocean were reflected, and while others saw it only as a mass of vapours given off by the earth, or as a revolving globe which was half fire and half ice, a few learned men, using observations in default of optical instruments, deduced most of the laws governing the Queen of the Night.

Thus Theles of Miletus, in 460 B.C., expressed the opinion that the moon was illuminated by the sun. Aristarchus of Samos gave an accurate explanation of its phases. Cleomedes taught that it shone with reflected light. Then Chaldean Berosus discovered that the duration of its rotation was equal to that of its revolution, and was thus able to explain the fact that it always presents the same side to our view. Finally Hipparchus, two centuries before the Christian era, distinguished a number of irregularities in the apparent movements of the earth's satellite.

These various observations were subsequently confirmed, and proved helpful to later astronomers. Ptolemy in the second century, and the Arab Abul Wefa in the tenth, completed Hipparchus's remarks on the irregularities of the moon's movements as it follows the undulating line of its orbit under the influence of the sun. Then Copernicus in the fifteenth century, and Tycho Brahe in the sixteenth, put forward a complete explanation of the solar system and of the part played by the moon in the host of heavenly bodies.

By this time its movements were more or less accurately established, but little was known of its physical constitution. It was then that Galileo explained the light phenomena produced in certain phases of the moon by the existence of mountains on its surface, giving the average height of these mountains as 27,000 feet.

Later on Hevelius, a Danzig astronomer, lowered the figure for the highest mountains to 15,600 feet, but his colleague Riccioli raised it again to 42,000 feet.

At the end of the eighteenth century Herschel, armed with a powerful telescope, greatly reduced the previous estimates. He put the height of the highest mountains at 11,400 feet, and brought down the average height to only 2,400 feet. But Herschel too was mistaken, and it took the observations of Schroeter, Louville, Halley, Nasmyth, Bianchini, Pastorf, Lohrman and Gruithuysen, and particularly the patient studies of Beer and Mädler, to settle the question for good. Thanks to these scientists, the height of the mountains on the moon is now known exactly. Beer and Mädler measured 1,905 mountains, of which six are over 15,600 feet in height, and twenty-two over 14,400 feet. Their tallest peak rises 22,806 feet above the moon's surface.

At the same time the telescopic exploration of the moon was being completed. The satellite appeared to be riddled with craters and its essentially volcanic character became increasingly obvious with every succeeding observation. From the absence of refraction in the rays from the planets hidden by it, scientists concluded that it must have practically no atmosphere. This absence of air implied an absence of water. It therefore became obvious that, in order to live in such conditions, the inhabitants of the moon must have a special constitution and be entirely different from the inhabitants of the earth.

Finally, thanks to the new methods, improved instruments

scanned the moon constantly, leaving no part of its visible surface unexplored, even though its diameter is 2,150 miles, rather more than a quarter of the earth's radius, its surface area one-thirteenth that of the earth, and its volume one forty-ninth. None of these secrets was able to escape the eyes of the astronomers, and those skilled scientists carried their amazing observations even further.

Thus they noticed that while the moon was full parts of it were streaked with white lines, and that during the phases it was streaked with black lines. They made a closer examination of these lines and succeeded in determining their precise nature. They were long narrow furrows with parallel edges, generally ending up at a crater; and they were about five thousand feet wide and anything between ten and a hundred miles long. The astronomers called them 'grooves', but giving them that name was all they were able to do. As for the question of whether or not these grooves were the dried-up beds of old rivers, they could not answer it satisfactorily. The Americans hoped to solve this geological mystery sooner or later. They also intended to reconnoitre that series of parallel ramparts discovered on the surface of the moon by Gruithuysen, a learned Munich professor, who believed them to be a system of fortifications erected by lunar engineers. These two obscure points, and doubtless many others, could not be definitely settled until direct communication had been established with the moon.

As for the intensity of its light, there was nothing more to be learnt in that respect: the scientists knew that it is three hundred times weaker than that of the sun, and that its heat has no perceptible effect on our thermometers. As for the phenomenon known by the name of 'ashen light', it can be explained by the effect of the sun's rays reflected from the earth to the moon, which seem to complete the lunar disk when it appears as a crescent during its first and last phases.

Such was the sum of knowledge which had been acquired about the earth's satellite, and which the Gun Club proposed to complete from every point of view: cosmographic, geological, political and moral.

6

What it is impossible not to know and what it is no longer permissible to believe in the United States

THE immediate result of Barbicane's announcement had been to draw the public's attention to all the astronomical facts relating to the Queen of the Night. Everybody set to work to study it assiduously. It was as if the moon had just appeared on the horizon for the first time and that nobody had ever caught sight of it in the sky before. It became the fashionable celebrity of the day without losing anything of its previous modesty, and took its place among the 'stars' without showing any more pride. The newspapers revived all the old stories in which the 'wolves' sun' played a part; they recalled the influence which the ignorance of past ages had attributed to it; they sang its praises in every possible key; with a little encouragement they would have started quoting its witty remarks. The whole of America went mad about the moon.

For their part, the scientific journals dealt more especially with those questions which touched upon the Gun Club's project. They published the letter from the Cambridge Observatory, commented on it and gave it their unreserved approval.

In short, it was no longer permissible for even the least learned of Americans to be ignorant of a single one of the facts relating to the satellite, or for even the most stupid of old women to go on holding superstitious beliefs about it. Science came to them in every conceivable form; it entered into them through their eyes and ears. It was impossible to be an ignoramus any more—in astronomy at least.

Until then, many people had not known how the distance

from the earth to the moon had been measured. The pundits took the opportunity to tell them that it had been obtained by measuring the moon's parallax. If the word 'parallax' seemed to surprise them, they were told that it was the angle formed by two straight lines projected to the moon from each end of the earth's radius. If they expressed doubts as to the accuracy of this method, they were immediately given proof that not only was this average distance 234,247 miles, but that the astronomer's error was less than seventy miles.

For the benefit of those who were not familiar with the movements of the moon, the newspapers demonstrated every day that it has two distinct movements, the first rotation on its axis and the second revolution around the earth, which each take the same length of time, namely twenty-seven and a third days.[1]

The movement of rotation is the one which creates day and night on the surface of the moon; but there is only one day and one night in every lunar month, and each lasts $354\frac{1}{3}$ hours. However, fortunately for the moon, the side facing the earth is illuminated by it with an intensity equal to the light of fourteen moons. As for the other side, which is always invisible to us, it naturally has $354\frac{1}{3}$ hours of utter darkness, mitigated only by 'the pale glow which falleth from the stars'. This phenomenon is due solely to the fact that the movements of rotation and revolution take place in precisely the same span of time, a phenomenon which, according to Cassini and Herschel, is common to Jupiter's satellites, and very probably to all other satellites too.

A few well-meaning but somewhat slow-witted persons were unable at first to understand that if the moon invariably showed the same side to the earth during its revolution, that was because during the same period it rotated once on its axis. They were told: 'Go into your dining-room and walk around the table while keeping your face turned towards the centre of it. By the time you have walked all the way round it you will have

[1] This is the duration of the sidereal revolution, i.e. the time the moon takes to return to a given star.

rotated once on your axis too, since your gaze will have passed over every point in the room. Well, the room is the sky, the table is the earth and you are the moon!' And they went away delighted with the comparison.

Thus the moon always shows the same side to the earth; although, to be more precise, it must be added that as a result of a certain oscillation from north to south and from west to east known as 'libration', it allows rather more than half of its disk—about 57 per cent—to be seen.

Once the ignorant had come to know as much as the director of the Cambridge Observatory about the moon's rotatory movement, they began to puzzle their brains over its revolutionary movement around the earth, and a score of scientific journals lost no time in enlightening them. They were told that the firmament, with its infinity of stars, can be regarded as a vast dial over which the moon moves, indicating the correct time to all the earth's inhabitants; that it is in this movement that the Queen of the Night exhibits her different phases; that the moon is full when it is in opposition to the sun, in other words when the three heavenly bodies are on the same straight line, with the earth in the middle; that the moon is new when it is in conjunction with the sun, in other words when it is between the sun and the earth; and finally that the moon is in its first or last quarter when it forms a right angle with the sun and the earth, with itself at the vertex.

A few perspicacious Americans concluded from these facts that eclipses could only occur at times of conjunction or opposition, and their reasoning was very sound. In conjunction the moon can eclipse the sun, while in opposition the earth can eclipse the moon, and if these eclipses fail to occur twice every lunar month that is because the plane on which the moon moves is inclined to the ecliptic, in other words the plane on which the earth moves.

As for the height which the Queen of the Night can attain above the horizon, the letter from the Cambridge Observatory had said everything there was to be said on that subject. Everybody knew that this height varies according to the latitude of the point of observation. But the only zones of the earth in which the moon passes the zenith, in other words the position directly above the observer, necessarily lie between the twenty-eighth parallels and the equator, Hence the important recommendation from the Cambridge Observatory to try the experiment at some point in this area of the earth, so that the projectile might be fired perpendicularly and thus escape more speedily from the force of gravity. This was an essential condition for the success of the enterprise, and the public were keenly alive to its importance.

As for the path followed by the moon in its revolution around the earth, the Cambridge Observatory had made it sufficiently clear, even to the ignoramuses of this world, that this path is a re-entrant curve, not a circle but an ellipse, with the earth occupying one of the foci. These elliptical orbits are common to all planets as well as to all satellites, and rational mechanics prove conclusively that this is inevitable. It was generally understood that the moon is farthest from the earth when it is at apogee, and nearest to the earth when it is in perigee.

This then is what every American knew whether he liked it or not: what nobody could decently admit to being ignorant about. But if these basic principles were rapidly disseminated, a great many errors and certain unfounded fears proved less easy to uproot.

For example, a few good people maintained that the moon was a former comet which, while describing its elongated orbit around the sun, had happened to pass near the earth and had been held prisoner in its field of gravity. These drawing-room astronomers considered that this explained the fire-ravaged appearance of the moon, an irreparable misfortune for which they blamed the sun. However, when it was pointed out to them that comets have an atmosphere, whereas the moon has little or none, they were at a loss for a reply.

Others, who belonged to the breed of tremblers, expressed certain fears with regard to the moon. They had heard that, since the observations made in the days of the Caliphs, the speed of its revolutions around the earth had increased to some degree. From this they concluded, logically enough, that an acceleration of motion must imply a reduction in the distance between the two bodies, and that if this process continued indefinitely the moon would end up one day by colliding with the earth. However, they had to calm down and stop fearing for future generations when they were told that, according to the calculations of a famous French mathematician called Laplace, this acceleration was confined within a very narrow limit, and that a proportional dimunition of speed was bound to follow before long. In other words, the equilibrium of the solar system could not be disturbed in the centuries to come.

Finally, there came the third class of ignoramuses, the superstitious. These people are not content to be ignorant, they insist that they know things which are completely untrue, and about the moon they knew a great deal. Some of them regarded the moon's disk as a polished mirror by means of which people could see one another from various points of the earth and communicate their thoughts. The others claimed that out of a thousand new moons which had been observed, 950 had brought about noteworthy changes, such as cataclysms, revolutions, earthquakes, floods and so on. In other words they believed that the Queen of the Night exerted a mysterious influence on human destiny, and regarded the moon as the 'real counterbalance' of existence. They thought that every inhabitant of the moon was attached to every inhabitant of the earth by a sympathetic link; like Doctor Mead they maintained that the vital system was wholly dependent on the moon, stubbornly insisting that boys were usually born during the new moon and girls during the last quarter, and so on and so forth. But finally they were obliged to abandon these vulgar errors and to admit the truth. And if the moon, stripped of its influence, was diminished in the eyes of those who worshipped all that was powerful, and a few backs were turned on it, the vast majority spoke up in its favour. As for the Americans, their sole ambition was to take possession of this new continent in space and to plant on its highest peak the star-spangled banner of the United States.

D

7

Hymn to the cannon-ball

IN ITS memorable letter of 7th October, the Cambridge
Observatory had dealt with the problems from the astronomical
point of view; it was now a matter of solving it mechanically.
At this stage the practical difficulties would have seemed
insurmountable in any other country but America. There they
were regarded as just child's play.

Without wasting any time President Barbicane had nomi-
nated an executive committee from among the members of
the Gun Club. In the course of three meetings this committee
was to elucidate the three major questions of the cannon, the
projectile and the powder to be used. It was composed of four
members who were experts on these subjects: Barbicane himself, who had a casting vote in the event of a deadlock, General
Morgan, Major Elphiston and finally the inevitable J. T.
Maston, who was appointed to act as secretary.

On 8th October the committee met at President Barbicane's
house at 3 Republican Street. As it was essential that such a
serious discussion should not be disturbed by the cries of the
stomach, the four members of the Gun Club sat down at a
table covered with sandwiches and enormous teapots. J. T.
Maston immediately screwed his pen into his iron hook and
the meeting began.

Barbicane spoke first.

'Gentlemen,' he said, 'we have to solve one of the most
important problems in the science of ballistics, that noble

science which deals with the movement of projectiles, in other words of bodies launched into space by some kind of propellant, and then left to themselves.'

'Ah, ballistics, ballistics!' J. T. Maston exclaimed in a voice full of emotion.

'Perhaps it might have seemed more logical,' Barbicane went on, 'to devote this first meeting to a discussion of the cannon . . .'

'Yes, indeed,' agreed General Morgan.

'However,' Barbicane continued, 'after careful consideration it seems to me that the question of the projectile should take precedence over that of the cannon, and that the dimensions of the latter should be dictated by the dimensions of the former.'

'I beg permission to speak!' cried J. T. Maston.

Permission was granted with all the deference due to his magnificent past.

'My good friends,' he said in inspired accents, 'our president is right to give the question of the projectile priority over all others. This cannon-ball we are going to hurl at the moon is our messenger, our ambassador, and I beg your permission to consider it from a purely moral point of view.'

This novel way of considering a projectile aroused intense curiosity on the part of the other members of the committee, and they accordingly gave the closest attention to J. T. Maston's words.

'Gentlemen,' the latter went on, 'I shall be brief. I shall make no mention of the physical cannon-ball, the cannon-ball that kills, to consider only the mathematical cannon-ball, the moral cannon-ball. To my mind, the cannon-ball is the most magnificent manifestation of human power; it is in the cannon-ball that human power is expressed in its entirety; it was in creating the cannon-ball that man came closest to the Creator!'

'Hear, hear!' said Major Elphiston.

'For if God made the stars and the planets,' cried the speaker, 'man made the cannon-ball, that criterion of earthly velocities, that reproduction in miniature of the heavenly bodies wandering through space, which, when you come to think of it, are really nothing but projectiles themselves! God can claim credit for the speed of electricity, the speed of light, the speed of the stars, the speed of the comets, the speed of the planets, the speed of the satellites, the speed of sound, the speed of the wind! But we can claim credit for the speed of the cannon-ball, a hundred times greater than the speed of the fastest trains and horses!'

J. T. Maston was carried away with emotion; his voice took on lyrical accents as he sang this sacred hymn to the cannon-ball.

'Would you like some figures?' he asked. 'Well, here are some that speak volumes! Take the humble twenty-four-pounder. It may move 800,000 times slower than electricity, 640,000 times slower than light, and 73 times slower than the earth in its orbit around the sun, yet when it leaves the cannon its speed is greater than that of sound [1]; it travels 1,200 feet per second, 12,000 feet in 10 seconds, 14 miles a minute, 840 miles an hour, 20,100 miles a day; in other words at the same speed as a point on the equator in the earth's rotatory movement, or 7,336,500 miles a year. At that speed it would take eleven days to travel to the moon, twelve years to get to the sun, and 360 years to reach Neptune, at the farthest boundaries of the solar system. That's what that humble cannon-ball, the work of our hands could do! Just imagine what it will be like when we fire off a projectile at twenty times that speed, at a velocity of seven miles a second! Ah, wonderful cannon-ball, splendid projectile, I like to think that you will be received up there with the honours due to a terrestrial ambassador!'

Cheers greeted this high-sounding peroration, and J. T. Maston, deeply moved, sat down amid the congratulations of his fellow members.

'Now that we have paid ample tribute to poetry,' said Barbicane, 'let us get down to the matter in hand.'

---

[1] Thus when a man has heard the sound of a cannon being fired, he cannot be struck by the cannon-ball.

'We are all ears,' replied the members of the committee as each bit into his sixth sandwich.

'You all know the problem we have to solve,' the president went on. 'We have to give a projectile a velocity of 36,000 feet per second. I have reason to think that we shall succeed. But for the moment let us examine the speeds which have been obtained so far. General Morgan can enlighten us on that point.'

'All the more easily,' replied the general, 'in that I served on the Experiment Committee during the war. I can therefore tell you that Dahlgren's hundred-pounders, which had a range of over five miles, gave their projectiles an initial velocity of 1,500 feet per second.'

The Rodman Columbiad

'Good. And what about the Rodman Columbiad [1]?' asked the president.

'The Rodman Columbiad, which was tested at Fort Hamilton, near New York, fired a projectile weighing half a ton a distance of six miles, at a speed of 2,400 feet per second, a speed never obtained by Armstrong and Palliser in England.

'Oh, the English!' snorted J. T. Maston, shaking his formidable hook in the direction of the eastern horizon.

'So 2,400 feet per second is the maxium velocity attained so far?' asked Barbicane.

'Yes,' replied Morgan.

'I must say,' interrupted J. T. Maston, 'that if my mortar hadn't exploded . . .'

'Yes, but it did explode,' Barbicane replied with a soothing gesture. 'We must therefore take as our starting point that velocity of 2,400 feet per second. We have to increase it nearly twentyfold. Now, leaving discussion of the means of attaining that velocity for another meeting. I will ask you, gentlemen, to give your attention to the dimensions we must give the cannon-ball. I need scarcely say that this is no longer a matter of a projectile weighing only half a ton!'

'Why not?' asked the major.

'Because our cannon-ball,' J. T. Maston replied sharply, 'must be big enough to attract the attention of the moon's inhabitants, always supposing that they exist.'

'Yes,' said Barbicane, 'and also for a still more important reason.'

'What do you mean, Barbicane?' asked the major.

'I mean that it is not enough to fire off a projectile and then take no further notice of it; we must follow it all the way up to the moment when it reaches its target.'

'Really?' exclaimed the general and the major, somewhat surprised at this idea.

'Why, yes,' Barbicane went on with the air of a man con-

[1] This was the name the Americans gave to those huge engines of destruction.

vinced he is right; 'why, yes, otherwise our experiment will be inconclusive.'

'But in that case,' the major objected, 'you must intend to give this projectile the most enormous dimensions?'

'No. Please hear me out. As you know, optical instruments have been brought to a high degree of perfection. With certain telescopes we have managed to magnify objects six thousand times and to bring the moon to an apparent distance from the earth of forty miles. Now at that distance objects sixty feet wide are perfectly visible. If the magnifying power of our telescopes has been increased no further than that, it is because their clarity decreases as that power increases, and the moon, which is simply a reflecting mirror, doesn't give off enough light for us to be able to increase magnification beyond that point.'

'Well then, what do you mean to do?' asked the general. 'Give your projectile a diameter of sixty feet?'

'No.'

'Then do you mean to make the moon brighter?'

'Precisely.'

'That's amazing!' exclaimed J. T. Maston.

'Yes, amazingly simple,' replied Barbicane. 'Because if I succeed in reducing the density of the atmosphere through which the light of the moon has to travel, I will have made that light brighter, won't I?'

'Of course.'

'Well then, to obtain that result, all I need to do is install a telescope on some high mountain. And that is what we are going to do.'

'I surrender,' replied the major. 'You have a wonderful way of making everything seem so simple. . . . And what degree of magnification do you hope to obtain that way?'

'Forty-eight thousand. That will bring the moon to an apparent distance of only five miles, and an object will need to be only nine feet across to be visible.'

'Splendid!' cried J. T. Maston. 'So our projectile will be nine feet in diameter?'

'Precisely.'

'Allow me to point out, however,' said Major Elphiston, 'that it will still be so heavy that——'

'Oh, Major,' replied Barbicane, 'before discussing its weight, let me remind you that our forefathers performed wonders in that respect. Far be it from me to say that the science of ballistics has made no progress, but we ought to remember that astonishing results were obtained as far back as the Middle Ages. I might even add that they were more astonishing than ours.'

'I don't believe it!' cried Morgan.

'Can you back up what you say?' J. T. Maston asked sharply.

'Nothing could be easier,' replied Barbicane. 'I can give you some examples to support my statement. Thus at the siege of Constantinople by Mohammed II in 1543, stone cannon-balls were fired which weighed 1,900 pounds and must have been pretty large.'

'Good Lord,' exclaimed the major; '1,900 pounds is quite a weight!'

'At Malta, in the days of the Knights, a cannon at Fort Saint Elmo used to fire projectiles weighing 2,500 pounds.'

'Incredible!'

'Finally, according to a French historian, during the reign of Louis XI a mortar fired a bombshell which weighed only five hundred pounds; but that bombshell went all the way from the Bastille, a place where the insane imprisoned the sane, to Charenton, a place where the sane imprisoned the insane.'

'Very good!' said J. T. Maston.

'Since then, what have we done when you come to think of it? The Armstrong cannon fires a five-hundred-pound ball, and the Rodman Columbiad a projectile weighing half a ton. It seems therefore that what our projectiles have gained in range, they have lost in weight. Now, if we bend all our efforts in that direction we must surely be able, with the progress science has made, to multiply tenfold the weight of the cannon-balls of Mohammed II and the Knights of Malta.'

'That's obvious,' replied the major. 'But in that case, what metal do you intend to use for the projectile?'

'Cast-iron, of course,' said General Morgan.

'Cast-iron?' cried J. T. Maston, in accents of utter contempt. 'That's a very common metal for a cannon-ball that's going to the moon!'

'Let's not overdo it, old fellow,' said Morgan. 'Cast-iron will do well enough.'

'Well then,' Major Elphiston went on, 'since the weight of the cannon-ball will be proportional to its volume, a cast-iron ball nine feet in diameter will still be appallingly heavy!'

'If it's solid, yes; but not if it's hollow,' said Barbicane.

'Hollow? You mean it's going to be a shell?'

'A shell we can put messages inside,' said J. T. Maston, 'and samples of the things we produce here on earth!'

'Yes, a shell,' replied Barbicane. 'It has to be a shell; a solid cannon-ball nine foot across would weigh over two hundred thousand pounds, and that's obviously too heavy. However, as the projectile has to have certain stability, I propose to give it a weight of twenty thousand pounds.'

'Then how thick are its walls going to be?' asked the major.

'If we keep to the standard proportions,' said Morgan, 'a diameter of four feet will require walls at least two feet thick.'

'That would be far too thick,' replied Barbicane. 'You have to remember that it isn't going to be a cannon-ball intended to pierce armour-plating; so its walls need only be thick enough to stand up to the pressure of the gases emitted by the powder. This, then, is our problem: how thick must the walls of a cast-iron shell be to weigh only twenty thousand pounds? Our brilliant mathematician, the worthy Maston, will tell us that straight away.'

'Nothing could be simpler,' replied the committee's secretary.

As he spoke he wrote a few algebraic formulas on a sheet of paper. His pen scrawled a π here and an x^2 there. He even appeared to produce a certain cube root without batting an eyelid. At last he said:

'The walls will have to be no more than two inches thick.'

'Will that be enough?' asked the major with a dubious expression.

'No,' replied President Barbicane, 'of course not.'

'Well, then, what's to be done?' Elphiston asked with a puzzled expression.

'We'll have to use some other metal than cast-iron.'

'Copper?' asked Morgan.

'No, that's still too heavy. I have something better than that to suggest.'

'What's that?' asked the major.

'Aluminium,' replied Barbicane.

'Aluminium!' exclaimed the president's three colleagues.

'That's right, gentlemen. As you know, in 1854 a famous French chemist, Henry Saint-Claire-Deville, succeeded in producing aluminium in a solid mass. Well, that precious metal is as white as silver, as unchangeable as gold, as tough as iron, as fusible as copper and as light as glass. It's easy to work, it's widely distributed in nature, since alumina forms the basis of most rocks, it's three times lighter than iron, and it seems to have been created for the express purpose of providing us with the material for our projectile!'

'Three cheers for aluminium!' cried the secretary, who was always extremely noisy in his moments of enthusiasm.

'But, my dear president,' said the major, 'isn't aluminium very expensive to produce?'

'It used to be,' replied Barbicane; 'when it had just been discovered, a pound of aluminium cost between 260 and 280 dollars; then the price dropped to 27 dollars, and now it's only 9 dollars.'

'But 9 dollars a pound,' retorted the major, who never gave in easily, 'is still a terribly high price!'

'True, my dear major, but not beyond our means.'

'How much will the projectile weigh if we make it of aluminium?' asked Morgan.

'Here's the result of my calculations,' replied Barbicane. 'A cannon-ball nine feet in diameter with walls one foot thick would weigh 67,440 pounds if it were made of cast-iron. If it were made of aluminium its weight would be reduced to 19,250 pounds.'

'Splendid!' exclaimed Maston. 'That suits us perfectly.'

'Splendid! Splendid!' echoed the major. 'But don't you realize that at 9 dollars a pound that projectile will cost——'

'One hundred and seventy-three thousand, two hundred and fifty dollars. Yes, I'm fully aware of that. But have no fear, gentlemen; this enterprise of ours won't go short of money, I can tell you that.'

'Money will pour into our coffers!' said J. T. Maston.

'Well, what do you think of aluminium?' asked the president.

'Carried!' replied the other three members of the committee.

'As for the shape of the projectile,' Barbicane went on, 'that isn't important, because once it has left the earth's atmosphere it will find itself in the void. I therefore propose a round ball which will revolve on its own axis if it wants to, and behave just as it likes.'

Thus ended the first meeting of the committee. The question of the projectile had been settled for good, and J. T. Maston rejoiced at the idea of firing an aluminium cannon-ball at the inhabitants of the moon.

'That,' he said, 'will give them some idea of what the inhabitants of the earth are like!'

8

The story of the cannon

THE decisions taken at this meeting had a considerable impact in the outside world. A few timorous souls took fright at the idea of a 20,000-pound shell being launched into space. Others wondered what sort of cannon could ever give enough initial velocity to such a mass. These questions would be triumphantly answered by the minutes of the committee's second meeting.

On the evening after the first meeting the four members of the committee sat down at table before new mountains of sandwiches and on the shores of a positive ocean of tea. The discussion was promptly resumed, this time without any preamble.

'Gentlemen,' said Barbicane, 'we are now going to examine the question of the cannon we have to build—its length, shape, composition and weight. In all probability we shall have to endow it with gigantic dimensions; but however great the difficulties facing us may be, our industrial genius will easily overcome them. So please listen to me and don't hesitate to raise objections to anything I have to say. I'm not afraid of them.'

A murmur of approval greeted this statement.

'Allow me to remind you,' Barbicane went on, 'what point our discussion had reached yesterday. The problem facing us now is how to give an initial velocity of 36,000 feet per second to a shell with a diameter of nine feet and a weight of 20,000 pounds.'

'That's the problem all right,' said Major Elphiston.

'I'll go on from there,' said Barbicane. 'When a projectile is launched into space, what happens? It is acted upon by three independent forces: the resistance of the air, the pull of the earth's gravity, and the force of the impetus which the cannon has given it. Let us examine these three forces. The resistance of the air will be insignificant. Remember that the earth's atmosphere is only forty miles thick. Travelling at a speed of 36,000 feet per second, the projectile will go through it in five seconds, and this period is too brief for us to regard the resistance of the air as a significant factor. Let us go on to consider the pull of the earth's gravity, in other words the shell's weight. We know that that weight will diminish in inverse ratio to the square of the distance the shell has travelled from the earth. This, in fact, is what physics teaches us: when a body left on its own falls towards the surface of the earth, it falls fifteen feet in the first second, but if that same body were removed to a point 257,542 miles away, in other words as far away as the moon is, its fall would be reduced to only a fraction of an inch in the first second. That is to say, it would remain virtually motionless. Our task, therefore, is to overcome this gravitational pull by degrees. How are we to do that? By the force of the impetus we give the projectile.'

'That's the difficulty,' said the major.

'True,' replied the president, 'but we shall overcome it, for the impetus we need will be governed by the length of the cannon and the amount of powder we use, the latter being limited only by the strength of the cannon. Today, then, let us decide the dimensions we are going to give the cannon. Remember that to all intents and purposes we can make it as strong as we like, since there will be no need to move it.'

'That's all quite clear,' said the general.

'Up to the present time,' said Barbicane, 'the longest cannons in existence, our huge Columbiads, have not exceeded twenty-five feet in length; so we are going to surprise a lot of people with the dimensions we shall have to adopt.'

'We'll surprise them all right!' exclaimed J. T. Maston.

'Speaking for myself, I propose making the cannon at least half a mile long!'

'Half a mile!' the major and the general exclaimed in unison.

'Yes, half a mile, and even then it won't be half long enough.'

'Come now, Maston,' said Morgan, 'you're exaggerating.'

'No, I'm not,' retorted the hot-tempered secretary. 'I don't know how you can say such a thing!'

'I said it because you're going too far.'

'Let me tell you, sir,' J. T. Maston said loftily, 'that an artilleryman is like a cannon-ball: he can never go too far!'

Here the president intervened, seeing that the argument was taking a personal turn.

'Let's calm down, gentlemen, and work this out logically. We obviously need a very long cannon, because the length of the gun will increase the force of the gases accumulated behind the projectile, but there is no point in going beyond a certain limit.'

'Precisely,' said the major.

'Now what are the rules in such a case? Usually the length of the cannon is between twenty and twenty-five times the diameter of the cannon-ball, and it weighs between 235 and 240 times as much.'

'That isn't enough!' J. T. Maston exclaimed impetuously.

'I agree, my good friend, because applying that ratio to a projectile nine feet in diameter and weighing 20,000 pounds, the cannon would be only 225 feet long and would weigh only 4,800,000 pounds.'

'That's ridiculous!' cried J. T. Maston. 'We might just as well use a pistol!'

'I think so too,' replied Barbicane. 'That's why I propose we quadruple that length and make a cannon 900 feet long.'

The general and the major raised a few objections; none the less, this proposal, strongly supported by the secretary of the Gun Club, was finally adopted.

'Now,' said Elphiston, 'how thick shall we make the cannon's walls?'

'Six feet thick,' replied Barbicane.

'You surely aren't thinking of mounting a mass like that on a gun-carriage?' asked the major.

'That would be wonderful,' said J. T. Maston.

'But impracticable,' said Barbicane. 'No, I'm thinking of casting this cannon in the ground, binding it with rings of wrought iron, and finally surrounding it with a thick mass of stone and lime, so that it benefits from all the resistance provided by the earth around it. Once the gun has been cast, it will have to be carefully bored and tertiated to prevent any space between the projectile and the bore; like that, there will be no loss of gas, and the whole expansive power of the powder will be used to provide propulsion.'

'Hurrah!' cried J. T. Maston. 'Now we've got our cannon!'

'Not yet!' replied Barbicane, calming his impatient friend with his hand.

'Why not?'

'Because we haven't discussed its shape. Is it to be a cannon, a howitzer or a mortar?'

'A cannon,' replied Morgan.

'A howitzer,' answered the major.

'A mortar,' cried J. T. Maston.

Another heated argument was about to break out, with each man advocating his favourite weapon, when the president cut it short.

'Gentlemen,' he said, 'I'm going to put you all in agreement; our Columbiad is going to be a combination of all three of those firearms. It will be a cannon, since the powder chamber will have the same diameter as the bore. It will be a howitzer, since it will fire a shell. And, finally, it will be a mortar, since it will be aimed at an angle of ninety degrees and since, being unshakeably fixed in the ground without any possibility of recoil, it will give the projectile all the propulsive power it possesses.'

'Agreed, agreed,' replied the other members of the committee.

'Just one simple question,' said Elphiston. 'Will this cannon-howitzer-mortar be rifled?'

'No,' replied Barbicane. 'We shall need an enormous initial velocity, and, as you know, a cannon-ball leaves a rifled barrel less rapidly than it leaves a smooth-bore one.'

'That's true.'

'Well, we've got it this time!' repeated J. T. Maston.

'Not quite,' retorted the president.

'Why not?'

'Because we don't know yet what metal it's to be made of.'

'Let's decide that straight away.'

'That's what I was going to suggest.'

Each of the four members of the committee wolfed a dozen sandwiches, washed down with a large cup of tea, and the discussion was resumed.

'Gentlemen,' said Barbicane, 'our cannon has to be extremely strong, very hard, heatproof, waterproof and impervious to the corrosive action of acids.'

'There's no doubt about that,' replied the major, 'and as we shall have to use a vast amount of metal, we shan't have a wide range of metals to choose from.'

'Well then,' said Morgan, 'I propose that we make our Columbiad of the best alloy known to man so far, namely a hundred parts of copper, twelve of tin and six of brass.'

'I admit, gentlemen,' said the president, 'that that alloy has given excellent results; but in this case it would be too costly and extremely difficult to use. I therefore think that we should use an excellent material which is also cheap, such as cast-iron. Don't you agree, major?'

'Absolutely,' replied Elphiston.

'Cast-iron,' Barbicane went on, 'costs only a tenth as much as bronze, it's easy to cast in sand moulds and it can be worked quickly; so that it's economical in both money and time. What's more, it's an excellent material, and I remember that during the war, at the siege of Atlanta, there were some cast-iron cannons which fired a thousand shots each at twenty-minute intervals without coming to any harm.'

'Yes, but cast-iron is very brittle,' objected Morgan.

'True, but also very strong. Our cannon won't burst, I promise you that.'

'There's nothing disgraceful about a burst barrel,' J. T. Maston declared sententiously.

'Of course not,' replied Barbicane. 'Well, I am now going to ask our worthy secretary to work out the weight of a cast-iron cannon 900 feet long, with an inner diameter of nine feet and walls six feet thick.'

'Right away,' replied J. T. Maston.

Just as he had done the previous day, he wrote out his formulas with marvellous ease, and a minute later announced:

'That cannon will weigh 68,040 tons.'

'And at two cents a pound, how much will it cost?'

'It will cost 2,510,701 dollars.'

J. T. Maston, the major and the general looked at Barbicane uneasily.

'Well, gentlemen,' said the president, 'let me repeat what I said to you yesterday: don't worry, there'll be no shortage of cash!'

With this assurance from the president, the committee adjourned, after fixing its third meeting for the following evening.

E

9

The question of powder

THE question of powder remained to be dealt with. The public was waiting anxiously for news of this final decision. Now that the size of the projectile and the length of the cannon had been settled, how much gunpowder would be necessary to provide the necessary propulsion? That awe-inspiring substance, which man had somehow managed to master, was going to be called upon to play its part in hitherto unheard-of proportions.

It is generally agreed and often repeated that gunpowder was invented in the fourteenth century by a monk called Schwartz, who paid for his great discovery with his life. But it has now been almost conclusively proved that this story must be classed among the legends of the Middle Ages. Gunpowder was not invented by anyone, it is directly descended from the so-called 'Greek fire', which is likewise composed of sulphur and saltpetre. In the course of time that mixture, which was only a fuse composition, gradually became an explosive mixture.

But while scholars are perfectly aware of the truth about the origins of gunpowder, few people realize its mechanical power. Yet this must be understood in order to appreciate the importance of the question facing the committee.

A litre of gunpowder weighs about two pounds, and when ignited produces 400 litres of gas. On being released, and under the action of a temperature of 2,400 degrees, this gas occupies a volume of 4,000 litres. Thus the ratio of a given volume of gunpowder to the volume of gas produced by its combustion is

1 to 4,000. It is therefore easy to imagine the terrifying force of that gas when it is compressed in a space 4,000 times too small for it.

This was all well known to the members of the committee when they met the next day. Barbicane gave the floor to Major Elphiston, who had been in charge of the powder factories during the war.

'Gentlemen,' said the distinguished chemist, 'I'll begin with some incontrovertible figures which will serve as a basis for discussion. The twenty-four-pounder, about which our worthy secretary waxed so lyrical the day before yesterday, needs only sixteen pounds of powder to fire its ball.'

'Are you sure of that figure?' asked Barbicane.

'Absolutely certain. The Armstrong cannon uses only seventy-five pounds of powder for an 800-pound projectile, and the Rodman Columbiad uses only 160 pounds of powder to send its half-ton projectile six miles. These facts cannot be called in question, for I have taken them myself from the records of the Artillery Committee.'

'That's true,' said the general.

'Well,' the major continued, 'the conclusion to be drawn from these figures is that the amount of powder does not increase in proportion to the weight of the cannon-ball. Thus, while we needed sixteen pounds of powder to fire a twenty-four-pounder, and for ordinary guns we use an amount of powder equal to two-thirds of the weight of the projectile, this ratio is not constant. Work it out for yourself, and you will see that, for a cannon-ball weighing half a ton, instead of 333 pounds of powder, only 160 pounds are actually required.'

'What are you driving at?' asked the president.

'My dear major,' said J. T. Maston, 'if you take your theory to its logical conclusion, you'll end up declaring that when your cannon-ball is heavy enough, you won't need any powder at all.'

'My good friend Maston can even joke about serious matters,' retorted the major, 'but let me reassure him: I'm going to propose an amount of powder which will fully satisfy his pride as an artilleryman. But I insist on pointing out that during the war, the amount of powder used for the biggest cannons was reduced after a series of experiments to a tenth of the weight of the cannon-ball.'

'That's perfectly true,' said Morgan. 'But before deciding on the amount of powder necessary to fire off our projectile, I think it would be as well to agree on the kind we intend to use.'

'We shall use coarse-grained powder,' replied the major. 'It ignites faster than fine-grained powder.'

'I don't deny that,' retorted Morgan, 'but it's extremely disruptive and ends up by damaging a gun's bore.'

'Granted; but what is an undeniable disadvantage for a cannon intended for long service is no disadvantage for our Columbiad. We are running no risk of bursting the barrel, and the powder has to ignite instantaneously so that its mechanical effect may be as complete as possible.'

'We could make several priming-holes,' said J. T. Maston, 'to allow us to ignite the powder at various places at one and the same time.'

'True,' said Elphiston, 'but that would make the whole operation more complicated. So I'll return to my coarse-grained powder, which eliminates all these difficulties.'

'So be it,' replied the general.

'For his Columbiad,' the major continued, 'Rodman used a powder with grains as big as chestnuts, made of willow charcoal which was simply heated in cast-iron boilers. This powder was hard and shiny, and left no trace on the hand, contained a high proportion of hydrogen and oxygen, ignited instantaneously, and although extremely disruptive caused no perceptible damage to the barrel.'

'Well,' said J. T. Maston, 'it seems to me that there's no room for hesitation, and our choice is clear.'

'Unless you'd prefer gold powder,' the major added with a laugh, earning himself a threatening gesture from his touchy friend's iron hook.

Up to this point Barbicane had taken no part in the discussion, simply listening and letting the others do the talking. He had obviously got an idea of his own. Finally, he simply asked:

'Now, gentlemen, how much powder do you propose to use?'

The three other members of the committee glanced at one another for a moment.

'Two hundred thousand pounds,' Morgan said at last.

'Five hundred thousand,' said the major.

'Eight hundred thousand pounds!' cried J. T. Maston.

This time Elphiston did not dare to tax his fellow member with exaggerating. After all, it was a matter of sending a 20,000-pound projectile to the moon with an initial velocity of 36,000 feet per second. A brief silence accordingly followed the proposals made by the three men.

It was finally broken by Barbicane.

'Gentlemen,' he said in a calm voice, 'I am starting from the principle that our cannon, provided it is built in the proper conditions, will be of unlimited strength. I am therefore going to surprise my good friend Maston by describing his calculations as timid, and I propose to double his 800,000 pounds of powder.'

'Sixteen hundred thousand pounds?' cried Maston, jumping up and down in his seat.

'Precisely.'

'But in that case we'll have to come back to my idea of a cannon half a mile long.'

'That's obvious,' said the major.

'Sixteen hundred thousand pounds of powder,' the secretary of the committee went on, 'will occupy a volume of about 20,000 cubic feet. Now, as your cannon has a capacity of only 54,000 cubic feet, it will be half full, and the bore will not be long enough to enable the expanding gases to give the projectile sufficient velocity.'

There was no answer to that. J. T. Maston was telling the truth. Everyone looked at Barbicane.

'All the same,' the president went on, 'I insist on using that amount of powder. Just think of it: 1,600,000 pounds of powder will produce 6,000,000,000 litres of gas. Six thousand million! Imagine that!'

'Then what are we to do?' asked the general.

'It's very simple: we have to reduce that enormous amount of powder without reducing its mechanical power.'

'All right, but how do we do that?'

'I'll tell you,' Barbicane answered quietly.

The others gazed at him intently.

'Nothing, indeed,' he went on, 'could be easier than to reduce that mass of powder to a quarter of its volume. You are all familiar with that curious substance which forms the basic tissue of plants and is known as cellulose.'

'Ah,' said the major, 'now I understand you, my dear Barbicane.'

'This substance,' said the president, 'can be found in a state of absolute purity in various bodies, especially cotton, which is simply the fibres of the seeds of the cotton plant. Now cotton, when combined with cold nitric acid, is transformed into a substance which is highly insoluble, highly combustible and highly explosive. This substance was discovered some years ago, in 1832, by a French chemist called Braconnot, who called it xyloidine. In 1838 another Frenchman, a certain Pelouze, studied its various properties, and finally, in 1846, Schönbein, a professor of chemistry at Basel, suggested using it as a form of gunpowder. That powder is what we call gun-cotton . . .'

'Or pyroxylin,' said Elphiston.

'Or nitrocellulose,' said Morgan.

'Do you mean to say there wasn't a single American who can be given some credit for this discovery?' cried J. T. Maston, moved by a lively feeling of national pride.

'Not a single one, I'm afraid,' replied the major.

'All the same,' the president went on, 'I can comfort Maston by telling him that the work of one of our fellow countrymen can be linked with the study of cellulose, because collodion, which is one of the principal agents in photography, is simply pyroxylin dissolved in ether and alcohol, and it was discovered by Maynard, who was a medical student in Boston at the time.'

'Well, hurrah for Maynard and nitrocellulose!' cried the noisy secretary of the Gun Club.

'To get back to the subject of gun-cotton,' Barbicane went

on, 'you are all familiar with its properties, which are going to make it so valuable to us: it is child's play to prepare; you simply soak some cotton in smoking nitric acid for fifteen minutes, rinse it thoroughly in water, and let it dry.'

'Yes, nothing could be simpler,' said Morgan.

'What's more, gun-cotton is impervious to humidity—a valuable quality for our purposes, since it will take several days to load the cannon. It ignites at 170 degrees instead of 240, and it burns so quickly that it can be ignited on top of ordinary gunpowder without the gunpowder having time to catch fire.'

'Perfect,' said the major.

'However, it's more expensive than ordinary gunpowder.'

'What does that matter?' said J. T. Maston.

'Lastly, it can give a projectile a velocity four times greater than that given by ordinary powder. I should add that if it is mixed with a quantity of potassium nitrate equal to 80 per cent of its weight, its power is increased even further.'

'Will that be necessary?' asked the major.

'I don't think so,' replied Barbicane. 'So instead of 1,600,000 pounds of powder, we shall have only 400,000 pounds of gun-cotton; and as we can safely compress 500 pounds of gun-cotton into twenty-seven cubic feet, the whole charge will take up only 180 feet of the Columbiad's barrel. Like that the cannon-ball will have over 700 feet of bore to travel, with a force of 6,000,000,000 litres of gas behind it, before taking flight towards the Queen of the Night!'

At these eloquent words J. T. Maston found himself unable to contain his emotion: he threw himself into his friend's arms with the force of a projectile, and would have knocked a hole in him if Barbicane had not been built to stand up to any bombshell.

This incident brought the committee's third meeting to an end. Barbicane and his daring colleagues, to whom nothing seemed impossible, had just settled the complex problems of projectile, cannon and powder. Their plan had been drawn up, and nothing remained but to carry it out.

'That's just a detail, a mere trifle,' said J. T. Maston.

N.B.   In the course of this discussion, President Barbicane credits one of his fellow countrymen with the discovery of collodion. With all respect to the worthy J. T. Maston, this is a mistake, which has arisen from the similarity of two names.

It is quite true that in 1847 Maynard, then a medical student in Boston, hit on the idea of using collodion in the treatment of injuries, but collodion had been known since 1846. The honour of that great discovery belongs to a Frenchman, a very distinguished mind, a scholar who was at once a painter, a poet, a philosopher, a Hellenist and a chemist: Monsieur Louis Ménard.

10

One enemy to twenty-five million friends

THE American public was taking a lively interest in the smallest details of the Gun Club's project. It followed the committee's discussions day by day. The simplest preparations for the great experiment, the mathematical questions it raised, the mechanical difficulties which had to be solved, in short the whole operation filled it with frenzied excitement.

Over a year was to pass between the beginning of the work and its completion, but that period of time was not to prove devoid of thrills. The site to be chosen for the bore-hole, the construction of the mould, the casting of the Columbiad, and its extremely dangerous loading were more than enough to arouse the public's curiosity. Once the projectile was fired, it would be out of sight in a few tenths of a second; after that, only a privileged few would be able to see with their own eyes what would become of it, how it would behave in space and how it would reach the moon.

The result was that the public's chief interest lay in the preparations for the experiment and the exact details of its execution.

However, the purely scientific attraction of the operation was suddenly heightened by an unexpected incident.

We have already seen what hosts of admirers and friends Barbicane's project had won him. Yet, honourable and extraordinary as this majority was, it was not unanimous. One man, one solitary man in all the States of the Union, objected to the

Gun Club's experiment. He attacked it violently at every possible opportunity, and human nature is such that Barbicane was more deeply affected by that one man's opposition than by the applause of all the others.

Yet he was well aware of the motive of that antipathy, the origin of that solitary enmity, the cause of that long-standing personal animosity, and the vainglorious rivalry which had given rise to it.

. . . a bold, determined, violent man, a pure Yankee

The president of the Gun Club had never seen that persistent enemy of his. This was fortunate, for a meeting between the two men would have undoubtedly had deplorable consequences. That rival was a scientist like Barbicane, a proud, bold, determined, violent man, a pure Yankee. His name was Captain Nicholl, and he lived in Philadelphia.

Everybody knows about the curious struggle which arose during the American Civil War between guns and projectiles on the one hand and the armour-plating of naval warships on the other, with the former designed to pierce the latter, and the latter determined to resist the former. The result of this struggle was a radical transformation of the navies of both continents. Projectiles and armour-plating fought with unprecedented ferocity, the first growing larger and the second growing thicker in constant proportion. Warships armed with redoubtable guns went into battle under the cover of their invulnerable carapaces. Vessels such as the *Merrimac*, the *Monitor*, the *Tennessee* and the *Weckausen* fired huge projectiles after putting on armour against those of the enemy. They did unto others as they would not have had others do unto them, an immoral principle which is the basis of the whole art of war.

Now, while Barbicane was a great caster of projectiles, Nicholl was a great forger of armour-plating. The one cast night and day in Baltimore, while the other forged day and night in Philadelphia. Each pursued a line of thought fundamentally opposed to that of the other.

As soon as Barbicane invented a new cannon-ball, Nicholl invented a new type of armour-plating. The president of the Gun Club spent his life making holes, and Nicholl in pre-venting him from doing so. The result was a perpetual rivalry which eventually took on a personal character. Nicholl appeared in Barbicane's dreams as an impenetrable piece of armour-plating which he crashed into, and Barbicane appeared in Nicholl's dreams as a projectile which ran straight through him.

However, although they were following divergent courses these two scientists would have ended up by meeting each other, in spite of all the axioms of geometry—but then it would have been in a duel. Fortunately for these citizens who were so useful to their country, they were separated by a distance of fifty or sixty miles, and their friends placed so many obstacles on the road between them that they never met.

Now which of the two inventors had got the better of the

other was a matter of dispute; the results obtained made it difficult to come to a definite decision. However, it seemed that in the long run the armour-plating would have to give in to the cannon-ball. Nevertheless those who were competent to judge had their doubts on the subject. In some recent experiments, Barbicane's cylindro-conical projectiles had stuck like so many pins in Nicholl's armour-plating. That day the Philadelphia iron-forger thought he was victorious, and could not show enough contempt for his rival; but when the latter subsequently replaced the conical projectiles with ordinary 600-pound shells, the captain had to climb down. Although fired at only moderate velocity,[1] these projectiles cracked, pierced and completely shattered the finest armour-plating.

Matters had reached this point, and victory seemed to lie with the projectile, when the war came to an end on the very day that Nicholl finished a new type of armour-plating made of forged steel. It was a masterpiece of its kind, guaranteed to stand up to all the projectiles in the world. The captain sent it to the Polygon in Washington, challenging the president of the Gun Club to smash it. Barbicane, on the grounds that peace had been made, refused to try the experiment.

Infuriated by this answer, Nicholl offered to expose his armour-plating to the impact of projectiles of every imaginable sort, solid, hollow, round or conical. Again he met with a refusal from the president, who was clearly unwilling to compromise his latest victory.

Angered beyond belief by this unspeakable obstinacy, the captain tried to tempt Barbicane by giving him every possible chance. He offered to put up his armour-plating only two hundred yards from the cannon. Barbicane stood by his original refusal. A hundred yards? No, not even seventy-five.

'Fifty yards, then!' cried the captain through the medium of the newspapers. 'Twenty-five yards—and I'll stand behind my armour-plating!'

---

[1] The weight of the powder used was only a twelfth of the weight of the shell.

Barbicane replied that even if Captain Nicholl stood in front of it, he still would not shoot.

Nicholl could no longer restrain himself when he received this reply. He descended to personalities. He said that cowardice was cowardice, whatever form it took; that a man who refused to fire a cannon was very close to being afraid of it; that the artillerymen who now fought at a distance of six miles had prudently replaced personal courage with mathematical formulas; and that, furthermore, there was as much bravery in waiting calmly for a cannon-ball behind a sheet of armour-plating as in firing one under the proper conditions.

Barbicane made no reply to these insinuations; he may not even have known about them, for at that time he was completely absorbed in the plans for his great undertaking.

When the president made his famous speech to the Gun Club, Captain Nicholl's anger passed all bounds. It was mingled with extreme jealousy and a feeling of absolute impotence. How could he possibly invent something better than that 900-foot Columbiad? What armour-plating could ever withstand a 20,000-pound projectile? At first Nicholl was staggered, over-whelmed, stunned by that cruel blow; but then he recovered his strength and decided to crush the project beneath the weight of his arguments.

Accordingly he violently attacked the work of the Gun Club. He wrote a number of letters which the newspapers did not refuse to print. He tried to demolish Barbicane's plans scientifically. Once he had embarked on this fight, he resorted to all sorts of arguments, and it must be said that all too often they were specious and unsporting.

First, Barbicane was violently attacked in his figures; Nicholl tried to prove mathematically that his calculations were wrong, and he accused him of not knowing the basic principles of ballistics. Among other things, and going by his own calculations, he stated that it was absolutely impossible to give any object a velocity of 36,000 feet per second, and he maintained, algebra in hand, that even at that velocity such a heavy projectile would never get beyond the earth's atmosphere. It would not even reach a height of twenty miles! Furthermore, even assuming that the velocity could be attained, and that it would be sufficient, the shell would not stand up to the pressure of the gas produced by the combustion of 1,600,000 pounds of powder, and even if it should stand up to that pressure, it would not resist the temperature; it would melt as it left the Columbiad, and fall in a red-hot rain on the heads of the foolhardy spectators.

Barbicane ignored these attacks and went on with his work.

Then Nicholl tried a different approach. Without considering its uselessness from every point of view, he regarded the experiment as extremely dangerous both for the towns near the deplorable cannon and for the citizens who sanctioned such a reprehensible spectacle by their presence. He also pointed out that if the projectile did not reach its goal, which it could not possibly do, it would inevitably fall back to earth, and that the impact of such a mass, multiplied by the square of its velocity would cause great damage to some point on the globe. In such circumstances, with all due respect to the rights of free citizens, he felt that there were cases in which the intervention of the government was necessary, in order to prevent one man's caprice from endangering the safety of all.

Such were the extremes of exaggeration to which Captain Nicholl allowed himself to be driven. He was alone in his opinion, so no account was taken of his dire prophecies. He was allowed to shout himself hoarse, since that was what he wanted. He made himself the defender of a cause which was lost in advance. He was heard but not listened to, and he did not take a single admirer away from the president of the Gun Club, who in any case did not even bother to answer his rival's arguments.

Left without a leg to stand on, and unable to risk his life for his cause, Nicholl decided to risk his money. He therefore publicly announced in the *Richmond Enquirer* that he was willing to make the following series of wagers, arranged on an increasing scale:

1. That the Gun Club would not be able to obtain the funds necessary for its project $1,000

2. That the casting of a 900-foot cannon was impracticable and would not succeed $2,000

3. That it would be impossible to load the Columbiad, and that the gun-cotton would be prematurely ignited by the pressure of the projectile $3,000

4. That the Columbiad would burst the first time it was fired $4,000

5. That the projectile would not travel as far as six miles and would fall back to earth a few seconds after being fired $5,000

It can be seen that in his invincible obstinacy Captain Nicholl was risking a considerable sum: no less than $15,000.

Despite the size of the stake, on 19th October he received a sealed envelope containing this superbly laconic reply:

Baltimore, October 1

Done.

BARBICANE

I I

Florida and Texas

Meanwhile one matter remained to be decided: a favourable place had to be chosen for the experiment. According to the recommendations of the Cambridge Observatory, the projectile had to be fired perpendicular to the plane of the horizon, in other words, towards the zenith. Now the moon rises to the zenith only in places located between zero and twenty-eight degrees of latitude; that is to say, its declination [1] is only twenty-eight degrees. The Gun Club therefore had to choose the exact spot on the globe where the huge Columbiad would be cast.

On 20th October, at a general meeting of the Gun Club, Barbicane produced a copy of Z. Belltropp's magnificent map of the United States. But before he had time to unfold it, J. T. Maston asked for the floor with his usual vehemence and spoke as follows:

'Gentlemen, the matter we are going to deal with today is of truly national importance, and it will give us an opportunity to perform a great act of patriotism.'

The members of the Gun Club looked at one another without understanding what the speaker was driving at.

'None of you,' he went on, 'would ever dream of tampering with the glory of our country, and if there's one right that the

---

[1] The declination of a heavenly body is its latitude in the celestial sphere; its angular ascension is its longitude.

Union can claim, it's the right to have the Gun Club's redoubt-able cannon within its frontiers. Now, under the present cir-cumstances——'

'Good old Maston——' said Barbicane.

'Let me finish what I was saying,' the speaker went on. 'Under the present circumstances we are forced to choose a place fairly close to the Equator so that conditions will be right for our experiment——'

'If you don't mind——' said Barbicane.

'I demand free discussion of ideas,' retorted the impetuous J. T. Maston, 'and I maintain that the ground from which our glorious projectile will be launched must belong to the Union.'

'Of course!' cried several members.

'Well then, since our frontiers aren't wide enough, since the ocean constitutes an impassable obstacle to the south, and since we must seek that twenty-eighth parallel beyond the United States and in an adjacent country, we have a legitimate reason for fighting, and I demand that we declare war on Mexico!'

'No! No!' cried members all over the room.

'No?' said J. T. Maston. 'That's a word I'm surprised to hear within these walls!'

'But listen——'

'Never! Never!' cried the fiery orator. 'Sooner or later that war will be fought, and I demand that it be declared this very day!'

'Maston,' said Barbicane, firing his explosive bell, 'you no longer have the floor!'

Maston tried to make a retort, but a few of his colleagues succeeded in restraining him.

'I agree,' said Barbicane, 'that the experiment can and must take place only on the territory of the Union, but if my im-patient friend had had let me speak, if he had glanced at a map, he would know that there is no need whatever to declare war on our neighbours, because some frontiers of the United States extend beyond the twenty-eighth parallel. As you can see from this map, we have the whole southern part of Texas and Florida at our disposal.'

F

The incident was closed, but it was not without regret that J. T. Maston let himself be convinced. It was accordingly decided that the cannon would be cast in either Texas or Florida. But this decision was to stir up unprecedented rivalry between the towns of those two states.

When it meets the American coast, the twenty-eighth parallel crosses the Florida peninsula and divides it into two roughly equal parts. Then it plunges into the Gulf of Mexico, passes beneath the arc formed by the coasts of Alabama, Mississippi and Louisiana, cuts off one corner of Texas, extends across Mexico, crosses Sonora and Old California and heads into the Pacific. So only those portions of Texas and Florida below this parallel fulfilled the conditions of latitude recommended by the Cambridge Observatory.

Southern Florida has no large towns, only a sprinkling of forts built to give protection against wandering Indians. Only one town, Tampa, could put forward a claim to be chosen on the basis of its location.

In Texas, on the contrary, the towns are larger and more numerous. Corpus Christi in Nuecas County, all the towns on the Rio Bravo, such as Laredo, Comalites and San Ignacio in Webb County, Roma and Rio Grande City in Starr County, Edinburg in Hidalgo County, and Santa Rita, El Panda and Brownsville in Cameron County formed an imposing league against the claims of Florida.

As a result, the decision had scarcely been announced before delegates from Texas and Florida arrived post-haste in Baltimore. From then on, President Barbicane and the influential members of the Gun Club were besieged night and day by pressing demands. If seven Greek cities quarrelled over the honour of having been Homer's birthplace, two whole states now threatened to come to blows over a cannon.

These 'fierce brothers' were seen walking the streets of the city in armed groups. Every time they met there was a risk of a conflict which would have had disastrous consequences. Fortunately President Barbicane's caution and skill warded off this danger. Personal feelings were given an outlet in the newspapers of the various states. Thus the *New York Herald* and the *Tribune* supported Texas, while the *Times* and the *American Review* espoused the cause of the Florida deputies. The members of the Gun Club did not know which to listen to.

Texas proudly produced its twenty-six counties and seemed to line them up in battle array; Florida replied that its twelve counties could do more than twenty-six in a state which was six times smaller.

Texas bragged about its 330,000 inhabitants; Florida boasted that it was more densely populated with its 56,000 inhabitants, since its territory was far smaller. Furthermore it accused Texas of specializing in malaria, which cost it the lives of several thousand people every year. And what it said was true.

Texas retorted that Florida was second to none when it came to fevers, and that it was foolhardy, to say the least, to accuse other places of being unhealthy when it had the honour of having *vomigo negro* in a chronic state. And what it said was true.

'Besides,' the Texans added through the medium of the *New York Herald*, 'some consideration should be shown to a state which grows the best cotton in the country, produces the best green oak for shipbuilding, contains magnificent coal deposits and has iron mines whose yield is 50 per cent pure ore.'

To this the *American Review* replied that, while the soil of Florida was not as rich, it offered better conditions for moulding and casting the Columbiad because it was composed of sand and clayey earth.

'But,' said the Texans, 'before casting anything in a place, you have to get there first, and communications with Florida are difficult, while the coast of Texas has Galveston Bay, which has thirty-five miles of coastline and is big enough to hold all the fleets in the world.'

'You must be joking with your Galveston Bay,' replied the newspapers devoted to Florida, 'because it's above the twenty-ninth parallel. But we have Espiritu Santo Bay, which opens right onto the twenty-eighth parallel and enables ships to go directly to Tampa.'

'A fine bay!' retorted Texas. 'It's half silted up!'

'Silted up yourself!' cried Florida. 'Are you trying to insinuate that this is a land of savages?'

'Well, the Seminoles still roam across your prairies!'

'What about your Apaches and Comanches? I suppose you say they're civilized!'

The war had been going on like this for several days when Florida tried to draw its adversary on to fresh ground. One morning *The Times* hinted that since the project was 'thoroughly American', it should take place only on 'thoroughly American' land.

Texas was stung to the quick. 'American!' it cried. 'We're just as American as you are! Texas and Florida both became part of the Union in 1845!'

'Maybe,' said *The Times*, 'but we had belonged to the Americans since 1820.'

'You certainly had,' said the *Tribune*. 'After being Spanish or English for two hundred years, you were sold to the United States for five million dollars!'

'What of it?' retorted the Floridans. 'That's nothing to be ashamed of. Wasn't all the land in the Louisiana Purchase bought from Napoleon in 1803 for sixteen million dollars?'

'It's disgraceful!' cried the Texas deputies. 'A wretched scrap of land like Florida dares to compare itself to Texas, which, instead of selling itself, achieved its own independence by driving out the Mexicans on 2nd March 1836, declared itself a federal republic after Sam Houston's victory over Santa Anna's troops on the banks of the San Jacinto and later voluntarily joined the United States!'

'Because it was afraid of the Mexicans,' said Florida.

Afraid! This word was much too strong, and as soon as it was spoken the situation became intolerable. Everyone expected the two groups to slit each other's throats in the streets of Baltimore. The authorities were obliged to keep the deputies under surveillance at all times.

President Barbicane was at his wits' end. His house was inundated with notes, documents and threatening letters. What decision was he to make? From the standpoint of suitability of soil, ease of communication and speed of transport, the two states were evenly matched. As for political considerations they were completely irrelevant.

This hesitation and perplexity had lasted for a long time when Barbicane resolved to put an end to it. He summoned his colleagues to a meeting, and laid before them a proposal which was profoundly wise, as will be seen.

'In view of what has been happening between Florida and Texas,' he said, 'it is obvious that the same difficulties will arise among the towns of whichever state we choose. The rivalry will simply pass from the genus to the species, from the state to the town. Texas has eleven towns which meet all the necessary conditions, and if Texas is chosen, they will fight for the honour of having the project and create more trouble for us. But Florida has only one town, so I say: Florida and Tampa!'

When this decision was made public it was a crushing blow to the deputies from Texas. They flew into an indescribable rage and personally challenged every member of the Gun Club to a duel. Only one course of action was left to the Baltimore authorities, and they took it. A special train was chartered, the Texans were put aboard it whether they liked it or not, and they then left the city at a speed of thirty miles an hour.

Despite the speed of their departure, they still had time to hurl one last sarcastic and threatening remark at their adversaries.

Referring to the narrowness of the Florida peninsula, they claimed it would not be able to stand up to the shock of the discharge and would be blown to pieces the first time the cannon was fired.

'Then let it be blown to pieces!' the Floridans replied with a laconicism worthy of ancient times.

1 2

Urbi et orbi

ONCE the astronomical, mechanical and geographical difficulties had been solved, the question of money arose. An enormous sum had to be procured if the project were to be carried out. The necessary millions could not be provided by any individual, or even by any single state.

Therefore, although the project was an American undertaking, President Barbicane decided to make it a matter of worldwide interest by asking for the financial co-operation of every nation. It was both the right and the duty of the whole world to take a hand in the affairs of its satellite. The subscription which was opened for this purpose extended from Baltimore to the whole world, *urbi et orbi*.

This subscription was to succeed beyond all expectation, even though the money was donated, not lent. It was a purely disinterested operation in the strictest sense of the term and offered no chance of profit.

But the effect of Barbicane's announcement had not stopped at the frontiers of the United States; it had crossed the Atlantic and the Pacific, invading Asia, Europe, Africa and Oceania. The observatories of the Union immediately entered into communication with foreign observatories. Some of the latter —those in Paris, St Petersburg, Capetown, Berlin, Altona, Stockholm, Warsaw, Hamburg, Buda, Bologna, Malta, Lisbon, Benares, Madras and Peking—sent their congratulations to the Gun Club. The others maintained a prudent silence.

As for the Greenwich Observatory, supported by the twenty-two other astronomical establishments in Great Britain, it was absolutely explicit: it boldly denied the possibility of success, and stated its agreement with Captain Nicholl's theories. Thus, while various learned societies promised to send representatives to Tampa, the Greenwich staff held a meeting at which Barbicane's proposal was unceremoniously brushed aside. This was simply a case of English jealousy, and nothing else.

All considered, the reaction was excellent in the scientific world, and from there it passes to the masses, who, in general, were keenly interested in the project. This was a most important fact, since these masses were going to be called upon to subscribe a vast amount of money.

On 8th October President Barbicane had issued an enthusiastic manifesto in which he appealed to 'all men of goodwill on earth'. This document, translated into all languages, met with enormous success.

Subscriptions were opened in the main cities of the Union, with a central office in the Bank of Baltimore, at 9 Baltimore Street, and were also opened in various countries in Europe and America, with the following firms:

Vienna: S. M. Rothschild
St Petersburg: Stieglitz and Co.
Paris: Crédit Mobilier
Stockholm: Tottie & Arfuredson
London: N. M. Rothschild & Son
Turin: Ardouin & Co.
Berlin: Mendelssohn
Geneva: Lombard, Odier & Co.
Constantinople: the Ottoman Bank
Brussels: S. Lambert
Madrid: Daniel Weisweller
Amsterdam: the Netherlands Credit Bank
Rome: Torlonia & Co.
Lisbon: Lecesne & Co.
Copenhagen: the Private Bank
Buenos Aires: the Maua Bank
Rio de Janeiro: the same firm

Montevideo: the same firm
Valparaiso: Thomas la Chambre and Co.
Mexico City: Martin Daran & Co.
Lima: Thomas la Chambre & Co.

Within three days of the publication of President Barbicane's manifesto, four million dollars had been deposited in the different American cities. With such a first instalment, the Gun Club could set to work straight away.

A few days later dispatches arrived informing America that the foreign subscriptions had been eagerly taken up. Some countries had distinguished themselves by their generosity; others did not loosen their purse strings so easily. It was a matter of temperament.

Figures are more eloquent than words, so here is the official record of the sums which were credited to the account of the Gun Club after the subscription was closed:

For her share, Russia paid the enormous sum of 368,733 roubles. This will surprise only those readers who are unfamiliar with the Russians' strong scientific leanings and the progress they have made in astronomical studies, thanks to their many observatories, the most important one of which cost two million roubles.

France began by laughing at the Americans' pretentions. The moon served as a pretext for countless tired puns and a score of vaudevilles in which bad taste was combined with ignorance. But just as the French used to pay after having sung, they now paid after having laughed, and they subscribed the sum of 1,253,930 francs. At that price they were fully entitled to a little merriment.

Austria showed sufficient generosity in the midst of her financial troubles. Her share of the public contribution was 216,000 florins, which was a welcome sum.

Sweden and Norway contributed 52,000 rixdalers. This was a large sum in relation to the population, but it would certainly have been larger if the subscription had taken place in Christiania as well as in Stockholm. For one reason or another, the Norwegians do not like to send their money to Sweden.

Prussia showed her warm approval of the undertaking by sending 250,000 thalers. Her various observatories eagerly contributed a sizeable sum and were the most ardent in encouraging President Barbicane.

Turkey behaved generously, but she had a personal interest in the matter, for the moon governs the course of her years and her fast of Ramadan. She could scarcely do less than give 1,372,640 piasters, although she gave them with an eagerness which betrayed a certain pressure from the Ottoman Government.

Belgium distinguished herself among all the smaller countries by a gift of 513,000 francs, or about two centimes per inhabitant.

Holland and her colonies put 110,000 florins into the project, asking only that they be given a 5 per cent discount, since they were paying cash.

Although a little restricted in the way of territory, Denmark gave 9,000 ducats, which proves the Danes' love of scientific expeditions.

The Germanic Confederation agreed to give 34,285 florins. She could not have been asked for more than that; and anyway, she would not have given it.

Italy, although in straitened circumstances, managed to find 200,000 lire by turning her children's pockets inside out. If she had had Venetia she would have done better; but she did not have it.

The Papal States felt it incumbent on them to contribute no less than 7,040 scudi, and Portugal showed her devotion to science with a donation of 30,000 crusados.

As for Mexico, her gift amounted to only 86 piasters, but an empire which has just been founded is always a little hard up.

Switzerland's modest contribution to the American project was 257 francs. It must be said frankly that she did not see any practical point in the operation. It seemed unlikely to her that sending a cannon-ball to the moon would result in the establishment of business relations with the Queen of the Night, and she felt it would be imprudent to invest any capital in such a hazardous undertaking. And, after all, she may have been right.

As for Spain, it was impossible for her to get together more than 110 reals. She gave as her excuse that she had her railways to finish. The truth is that science is not very highly regarded in that country. It is still a little backward. Furthermore there were some Spaniards, not among the least educated, who did not have a clear idea of the relation between the mass of the projectile and that of the moon; they were afraid that the projectile might alter the moon's orbit, interfere with its role as a satellite and bring it crashing into the earth. Under such circumstances they felt it would be better to abstain, and, apart from donating a few reals, that was what they did.

There was still England. We have already mentioned the contemptuous hostility with which she greeted Barbicane's proposal. The twenty-five million people who live in Great Britain have only a single soul between them. They maintained that the Gun Club's project was contrary to the principle of non-intervention, and they refused to give a solitary farthing to it. On hearing this news, the members of the Gun Club shrugged their shoulders and went on with their great work.

When South America—that is, Peru, Chile, Brazil and Colombia—had given 300,000 dollars as her share, the Gun Club had a considerable amount of capital at its disposal: 4,000,000 dollars from the United States subscriptions and 1,410,143 dollars from the foreign subscriptions, making a grand total of 5,410,143 dollars.

Such was the sum the public poured into the treasury of the Gun Club. The size of this sum should not surprise anyone. According to the estimates, the money would be almost entirely absorbed by the work of casting and boring, masonry, transporting the workers and billeting them in an almost uninhabited region, constructing furnaces and buildings, equipping factories, the powder, the projectile and incidental expenses. During the American Civil War there had been cannon shots which cost a thousand dollars each; President Barbicane's shot, unique in the annals of artillery, could easily cost five thousand times as much.

On 20th October a contract was signed with the Goldspring

factory, near New York, which had supplied Parrott with his best cast-iron cannons during the war.

It was stipulated in the contract that the Goldspring factory assumed responsibility for transporting the material for the casting of the Columbiad to Tampa in Southern Florida. This operation was to be terminated by 15th October of the following year at the very latest, and the cannon was to be handed over in good condition, under penalty of an indemnity of a hundred dollars a day, until the next time when the moon would be in the same conditions, that is, in eighteen years and eleven days. The Goldspring Company would also be responsible for hiring and paying the workers, and making all the necessary arrangements.

Two copies of this contract were signed by I. Barbicane, president of the Gun Club, and J. Murchison, manager of the Goldspring factory, after both men had given their approval to its terms.

13

Stone Hill

AFTER the Gun Club had decided against Texas everybody in the United States, where there is nobody who cannot read, made a point of studying the geography of Florida. The bookshops had never sold so many copies of Bertram's *Travel in Florida*, Roman's *Natural History of East and West Florida*, Williams's *The Territory of Florida* and Cleland's *On the Cultivation of the Sugar-Cane in East Florida*. New editions had to be printed to satisfy the frenzied demand for information.

Barbicane had better things to do than read : he wanted to establish the site of the Columbiad and see it with his own eyes. Without wasting a single moment, he therefore turned over to the Cambridge Observatory the funds necessary for the construction of a telescope and negotiated a contract with Breadwill and Co. of Albany for the manufacture of the projectile in aluminium. He then left Baltimore, accompanied by J. T. Maston, Major Elphiston and the manager of the Goldspring Company.

They reached New Orleans the next day. There they immediately boarded the *Tampico*, a dispatch boat of the Federal Navy which the government had placed at their disposal. They left the harbour at full steam and the coast of Louisiana soon vanished behind them.

The voyage was not long. Two days after their departure, after covering 480 miles, they sighted the coast of Florida. As they approached it Barbicane saw that the land was low, flat and somewhat barren-looking. After passing a succession of coves rich in oysters and lobsters, the *Tampico* entered Espiritu Santo Bay.

This bay is divided into two long roadsteads, the Tampa roadstead and the Hillsboro roadstead, and the steamer soon entered the latter. A short time later the batteries of Fort Brooke came into view, then the town of Tampa appeared, nestling at the far end of the little natural harbour formed by the mouth of the Hillsboro River.

It was there that the *Tampico* dropped anchor on 22nd October, at seven o'clock in the evening. The four passengers immediately went ashore.

Barbicane felt his heart pounding as he set foot on Florida soil. He seemed to be testing it, like an architect testing the solidity of a house. J. T. Maston scratched the ground with the tip of his hook.

'Gentlemen,' said Barbicane, 'we have no time to lose. Tomorrow we'll set off on horseback to reconnoitre the region.'

As soon as Barbicane had stepped ashore the three thousand inhabitants of Tampa had come forward to meet him—an honour to which the president of the Gun Club was fully entitled for having favoured them with his choice. They received him with a formidable burst of cheering, but Barbicane escaped from this ovation to a room in the Franklin Hotel and refused to see anyone. The role of a famous man did not suit him at all.

The next day, 23rd October, a group of little Spanish horses, full of vigour and fire, were prancing beneath his windows. But instead of four, there were fifty, all with their riders. Barbicane and his three companions went downstairs. At first he was surprised to find himself in the midst of such a cavalcade. He also noticed that each rider had a rifle slung over his shoulder and a brace of pistols in his saddle holsters. The reason for such a display of armed strength was promptly given him by a young Floridan who said to him:

'It's because of the Seminoles, sir.'

'What are Seminoles?'

'They are savages who roam the prairies. We thought it would be better if we escorted you.'

'Ridiculous!' said J. T. Maston as he mounted his horse.

'Well, it's safer,' said the Floridan.

'Thank you for your thoughtfulness, gentlemen,' said Barbicane. 'And now, let's be off!'

The little troop set off immediately and vanished in a cloud of dust. It was five o'clock in the morning. The sun was already shining brightly and the temperature was eighty-four, but the heat was tempered by a cool sea breeze.

After leaving Tampa, Barbicane rode southwards, following the coast as far as Alifia Creek. This little river runs into Hillsboro Bay twelve miles below Tampa. Barbicane and his escort rode eastwards along its right bank. Soon the bay disappeared behind a rise in the ground and they could see nothing but the Florida countryside.

Florida is divided into two parts. The northern part is more populous and less wild than the other. Its capital is Tallahassee, and one of the main naval arsenals in the United States is at Pensacola. The other part, squeezed between the Atlantic and the Gulf of Mexico, is only a slender peninsula washed by the Gulf Stream, and a finger of land lost in the midst of a little archipelago, which is constantly being passed by the many ships going along the Bahama Channel. It is the advanced sentry watching for the violent storms which attack the Gulf. The state's area is 38,033,267 acres, among which Barbicane had to find one which was situated below the twenty-eighth parallel and suitable for his project; consequently, as he rode along, he carefully examined the configuration and composition of the ground.

Florida, discovered by Juan Ponce de Leon in 1512, on Palm Sunday, was first named *Pascha Florida*, or 'Beflowered Easter'. It did not deserve this charming name on its hot, arid coasts. But a few miles inland the nature of the terrain gradually changed, and the region showed itself to be worthy of its name. It was criss-crossed with a network of creeks, streams, rivers, ponds and little lakes, and looked very like Holland or Guiana. Then the land began to rise perceptibly and soon revealed its cultivated plains on which all sorts of northern and southern crops were flourishing, its vast fields where the tropical sun and the water conserved in the clay of the soil did most of the work of cultivation, and finally its fields of pineapples, sweet potatoes, tobacco, rice, cotton and sugar-cane, stretching away as far as the eye could see, displaying their wealth with carefree prodigality.

Barbicane seemed highly pleased to note the gradual rising of the ground. When J. T. Maston asked him why, he replied:

'My dear fellow, it is very important for us to cast our Columbiad on high ground.'

'To be closer to the moon?' asked the secretary of the Gun Club.

'No,' said Barbicane, smiling. 'What difference would a few feet make? But on high ground our work will be easier: we won't have to fight against water, so we won't need long, expensive casing. That's an important consideration when you're digging a shaft nine hundred feet deep.'

'You're right,' said the engineer Murchison. 'We must avoid water as much as possible during the digging. But if we do come across underground springs it won't bother us: we'll either change their course or pump them dry with our machines. We won't be digging a dark, narrow artesian well,[1] where the drill, the casing, the sounding-rod and all the other well-digger's tools have to work blindly. No, we'll be working in the open air, in broad daylight, with picks and mattocks, and with the help of blasting we'll make rapid progress.'

'Even so,' said Barbicane, 'if the elevation or the nature of the soil can save us the trouble of dealing with underground water, the work will be done faster and better. So let's try digging a few hundred yards above sea level.'

'You are right, Mr Barbicane, and unless I'm mistaken we'll find a suitable site before long.'

'I wish we were giving the first stroke of the pickaxe!' said the president.

---

[1] It took nine years to dig the Grenelle well; it is 1,794 feet deep.

'And I wish we were giving the last!' cried J. T. Maston.

'We'll get there, gentlemen,' replied the engineer, 'and believe me, the Goldspring Company won't have to pay you any indemnity for being late.'

'I hope not, for your sake!' said J. T. Maston. 'Do you realize that a hundred dollars a day for eighteen years and eleven days, which is how long it will be before the moon is in the same conditions again, comes to 658,100 dollars?'

'No, sir, we didn't realize that,' replied the engineer, 'and we don't need to be told.'

By ten o'clock in the morning the little troop had ridden a dozen miles. The fertile fields were giving place to a forest in which a wide variety of trees grew in tropical profusion. This almost impenetrable forest was composed of huge vines and pomegranate, orange, lemon, fig, olive, apricot and banana trees, whose fruit and blossoms rivalled one another in colour and scent. In the fragrant shade of these magnificent trees a host of brightly coloured birds were singing and flying, the most striking of them all being the boatbills, whose nest should be a jewel case in order to be worthy of such feathered gems.

J. T. Maston and the major could not find themselves in such an opulent setting without admiring its magnificent beauties. But President Barbicane was insensitive to these wonders and was impatient to move on. This fertile region displeased him because of its very fertility; although he was not a water diviner, he could sense water beneath his feet, and he looked in vain for signs of incontestable dryness.

They rode on. They had to ford several rivers, and this was not without danger, for the water was infested with alligators fifteen to eighteen feet long. J. T. Maston boldly threatened them with his redoubtable hook, but he succeeded in frightening only the pelicans, garganeys, phaetons and other wild inhabitants of those parts, while big red flamingos stared stupidly at him.

Finally these denizens of the rain forests disappeared in their turn. The trees became smaller and less numerous, until finally there were only isolated clumps of them in the midst of vast

They had to ford several rivers, and this was not without danger

plains where startled herds of deer raced past.

'At last!' cried Barbicane, standing up in his stirrups. 'Here's a region of pine trees!'

'And savages too,' said the major.

A few Seminoles had appeared on the horizon. They rode excitedly back and forth on their swift horses, brandished long spears and fired muffled rifle shots, but they confined themselves to these hostile demonstrations. Barbicane and his companions were not alarmed.

They were now in the middle of a vast, rocky, sun-drenched space several acres in area. It was a sort of broad plateau and seemed to offer all the conditions required for the site of the Gun Club's Columbiad.

'Halt!' said Barbicane, reining his horse. 'Does this place have a name?'

'It's called Stone Hill,' replied one of the Floridans.

Barbicane dismounted without a word, took his instruments and began determining his position with extreme precision. Gathered around him, the little troop watched him in profound silence.

The sun was just then passing the meridian. A few moments later Barbicane quickly calculated the results of his observations and said:

'This site is 1,800 feet above sea level, latitude 27° 7′ north, longitude 5° 7′ west.[1] Its barren, rocky character seems to indicate all the conditions favourable to our project; so it is on this plateau that we shall build our powder magazines, our workshops, our furnaces and the houses for our workers, and it will be from here, from this very spot,' he repeated, stamping his foot on the summit of Stone Hill, 'that our projectile will take flight into the limitless regions of the solar system!'

[1] From the meridian of Washington

14

Pick and trowel

THAT same evening Barbicane and his companions returned to Tampa, and the engineer Murchison went back on board the *Tampico* to go to New Orleans. He was to hire an army of workers and bring back the greater part of the material. The two officials of the Gun Club remained in Tampa to organize the preliminary work with the aid of the local people.

Eight days after her departure, the *Tampico* came back into Espiritu Santo Bay with a fleet of steamships. Murchison had collected fifteen hundred workers. In the evil days of slavery he would have wasted his time and trouble, but now that America, the land of freedom, had only free men within her frontiers, they were willing to go wherever there were well-paid jobs. The Gun Club was not short of money; it offered its men high wages and generous bonuses. Any man who signed on to work in Florida could count on a large sum of money being deposited in his name in the Bank of Baltimore when the project was completed. Murchison accordingly had a wide choice and was able to set a high standard of intelligence and skill for his workers. There is every reason to believe that he filled his laborious legion with the finest mechanics, firemen, smelters, smiths, miners, brickmakers and labourers all sorts, black and white, without distinction of colour. Many of them brought their families with them. It was a positive emigration.

On 31st October, at ten o'clock in the morning, this troop disembarked on the quays of Tampa. It is easy to imagine the agitation and activity which reigned in that little town, whose population had been doubled in one day. Tampa was to gain enormously from the Gun Club's project, not because of the workers, who were immediately taken to Stone Hill, but because of the influx of sightseers who gradually converged on the Florida peninsula from all parts of the world.

The first few days were spent unloading the equipment brought by the fleet, machines, food supplies and a fairly large number of corrugated-iron houses divided into numbered pieces. At the same time, Barbicane began laying out a fifteen-mile railway between Tampa and Stone Hill.

The way in which an American railway is constructed is well known: capricious in its meanderings, bold in its slopes, despising barriers and works of art, climbing hills and plunging into valleys, it runs along blindly, with no concern for straight lines. It is neither costly nor troublesome, but its trains jump the track with reckless abandon. The line from Tampa to Stone Hill was only a trifle and required little time and money for its construction.

Barbicane was the life and soul of that community of people who had answered his call. He communicated his ardour, energy, enthusiasm and conviction to them. He seemed to be everywhere at once, as if he were endowed with the gift of ubiquity, and he was always followed by J. T. Maston, his buzzing fly. His practical mind turned out a host of ingenious inventions. With him there were no obstacles, no difficulties, no complications; he was not just an artilleryman, but a miner, a mason and a mechanic as well, with an answer to every question and a solution to every problem. He carried on an active correspondence with the Gun Club and the Goldspring Company; and day and night, with a full head of steam, the *Tampico* awaited his orders in the Hillsboro roadstead.

On 1st November he left Tampa with a detachment of workers. The very next day, a town of iron houses rose around Stone Hill. A stockade was built around it, and from its bustle and animation it might have been one of the biggest cities in the Union. Life in it was regulated by a disciplinary system, and work began in perfect order.

After careful drillings had revealed the nature of the soil, digging began on 4th November. On that day Barbicane called his foremen together and said to them:

'Friends, you all know why I've brought you to this wild part of Florida. We're going to cast a cannon with an inside diameter of nine feet and walls six feet thick, surrounded by a stone revetment nineteen and a half feet thick: so the shaft we're going to dig will be sixty feet wide and nine hundred feet deep. This huge job has to be finished in eight months. You'll have to excavate 2,543,400 cubic feet of earth in 255 days, or, in round figures, 10,000 cubic feet a day.

'That wouldn't be hard for a thousand men working with plenty of elbow room; it won't be easy in a comparatively restricted space. But since it must be done, it will be done, and I'm counting on your courage as much as your skill.'

At eight o'clock in the morning the first pickaxe struck the soil of Florida, and from then on that valiant tool was never idle for a moment in the hands of the miners. The workers relieved each other every six hours.

However colossal the operation may have been, it was not beyond the capacity of human strength; far from it. How many undertakings of far greater difficulty, in which the elements had to be fought tooth and nail, have been brought to completion! To mention only similar projects, there was 'Father Joseph's Well', dug near Cairo by Sultan Saladin at a time before machines had increased man's strength a hundredfold: it descends three hundred feet below the level of the Nile. Then there was the six-hundred-foot well dug at Coblentz by Margrave Johann of Baden. All that Barbicane's men had to do was to triple the depth of Saladin's well and make it ten times wider, which would make digging easier. There was not one foreman or labourer who had any doubt about the success of the operation.

The work was speeded up by an important decision made by the engineer Murchison, with President Barbicane's approval.

A clause in the contract specified that the Columbiad was to be reinforced by bands of wrought iron put in place while they were still hot. This was a useless precaution, for it was obvious that the cannon could do without those rings. The clause was accordingly cancelled. This made it possible to save a great deal of time, for they were now able to use the new system of digging which has been adopted for wells, in which the masonry is made at the same time as the hole. Thanks to this simple process, it is no longer necessary to shore up the earth with braces: the masonry contains it with unshakeable strength, and moves down by its own weight.

This operation was not to begin until the digging had reached the solid part of the ground.

On 4th November fifty workers dug a circular hole sixty feet across at the centre of the stockaded enclosure, that is, at the top of Stone Hill.

First the pickaxe encountered a six-inch layer of black vegetable mould which it went through easily. Then came two feet of fine sand which was carefully taken out, for it was to be used in making the inner mould.

After this sand appeared four feet of compact white clay which resembled marl in England.

Then the picks struck sparks from the hard subsoil, a kind of dry, firm rock composed of petrified seashells, which they would have to contend with until the end of the digging. At this point the hole was six and a half feet deep, and the masonry work was begun.

At the bottom of this excavation they built an oak disk, firmly bolted and enormously strong, with a hole in the middle with the same diameter as the outer diameter of the Columbiad. It was on this disk that they built the first courses of masonry, whose stones were held together with inflexible tenacity by hydraulic cement. When the workers had built stonework from the circumference to the inner circle, they were enclosed in a round pit twenty-one feet across.

Once this task had been completed, the miners took up their picks and mattocks again and began digging under the

disk, taking care to support it with extremely strong blocks.
Each time the hole had gone two feet deeper, they successively
took out these blocks; the disk would then gradually sink,
taking with it the massive ring of stonework on top of which
the masons were constantly working, not forgetting to leave
vent-holes through which the gas could escape during the
casting operation.

This sort of work required great skill and unremitting
attention on the part of both miners and masons. More than
one worker was seriously or even fatally injured by flying
splinters of stone while digging under the disk. But their ardour
never flagged for one minute, day or night. During the day, by
the light of a sun which raised the temperature of that scorched

*By the end of the first month the shaft had reached its scheduled depth
of 112 feet*

plain to ninety-nine degrees a few months later, and at night, by the white glare of electric lights, the noise of picks striking rock, the explosion of blasting charges, the grinding of machinery, and wreaths of smoke in the air created around Stone Hill a circle of terror which neither herds of buffalo nor groups of Seminoles dared to cross.

Meanwhile the work progressed steadily. Steam cranes speeded the removal of earth. There was little trouble from unexpected obstacles. Only difficulties which had been foreseen were encountered, and they were skilfully overcome.

By the end of the first month the shaft had reached its scheduled depth of 112 feet. In December this depth was doubled, and in January it was tripled. During the month of February the workers had to contend with an underground spring which welled up from beneath the surface. Powerful pumps and compressed-air equipment had to be used to draw off this spring in order to stop up its opening with concrete just as one stops up a leak in a ship. Finally these undesirable currents were mastered. But because of the looseness of the earth, the disk sank on one side and there was a partial collapse of the stonework. Imagine the terrifying weight of that ring of masonry 450 feet high! This accident cost the lives of several workers.

It took three weeks to shore up the stone revetment, build a support beneath it, and restore the disk to its original firm position. But thanks to the skill of the engineers and the power of the machines employed, the edifice recovered its balance and the excavation continued.

The work was not interrupted by any other incidents, and on 10th June, twenty days before the date set by Barbicane, the shaft, completely sheathed in its stone revetment, reached its scheduled depth of nine hundred feet. At the bottom the stonework rested on a massive thirty-foot cube, while its top was level with the surface of the ground.

President Barbicane and the other members of the Gun Club warmly congratulated the engineer Murchison. His Herculean task had been carried out with extraordinary speed.

During these eight months, Barbicane had not left Stone Hill for one moment. Keeping a close watch on the digging operations, he had been constantly concerned with the welfare and health of his workers, and he was lucky enough to avoid those epidemics which are common to aggregations of men, and are so disastrous in those regions of the world exposed to tropical influences.

Several workers, it is true, paid with their lives for the rashness inherent in such dangerous work; but these deplorable accidents are impossible to avoid, and Americans are not in the habit of worrying about such details. They care more about mankind in general than about the individual in particular. Barbicane professed contrary principles, however, and applied them at every opportunity. Because of his care, his intelligence, his useful intervention in difficult cases and his prodigious, humane sagacity, the accident rate did not go beyond that of European countries noted for their abundant precautions, including France, where there is an average of one accident for every 200,000 francs' worth of work.

15

The casting festival

DURING the eight months which were spent on the excavation, the preparatory work for the casting had been carried out simultaneously and with great speed. A stranger arriving at Stone Hill would have been amazed by what he saw.

Arranged in a circle around the shaft at a distance of 600 yards were 1,200 reverberatory furnaces six feet wide and three feet apart. The circumference of this circle of 1,200 furnaces was over two miles. They were all built to the same design, with a high rectangular chimney, and they produced a most curious effect. J. T. Maston felt that it was a magnificent architectural arrangement. It reminded him of the monuments of Washington. In his opinion there was nothing more beautiful anywhere in the world, not even in Greece, where, he admitted, he had never been.

It will be remembered that at its third meeting the committee had decided to use cast-iron, and in particular the so-called grey variety, to make the Columbiad. This metal is tougher, more ductile, more malleable and easier to bore than any other, and suitable for all casting operations. Smelted with coal, it is of superior quality for things that require great strength, such as cannons, steam-engine cylinders, hydraulic presses, etc.

But it is rarely homogeneous enough when it has been smelted only once. It takes a second smelting to purify and refine it by ridding it of all its earthy residues.

Therefore, before being sent to Tampa, the iron ore, smelted in the blast furnaces at Goldspring and placed in contact with heated carbon and silicon, was carburized, and transformed into cast-iron.[1] After this operation, the metal was sent to Stone Hill. But 135,000,000 pounds of cast-iron were involved, and this mass would have been too expensive to send by rail: the transport charges would have doubled the cost of the iron. It seemed preferable to charter ships in New York and load them with the iron in bars. It took no less than sixty-eight ships with a capacity of a thousand tons each, a real fleet. On 3rd May they left New York Harbor, headed out to sea, moved southwards along the coast to the Bahama Channel, rounded the tip of the peninsula, steamed into Espiritu Santo Bay on 10th May and all moored in the port of Tampa without incident. There the iron was unloaded from the ships and placed in the wagons of the Stone Hill railway. By the middle of January the enormous mass of metal had reached its destination.

It will be readily understood that the 1,200 furnaces were not too many to melt that 60,000-ton mass of metal all at once. Each furnace could contain about 114,000 pounds of metal. They had been made on the same pattern as those which had been used in casting the Rodman cannon: they had a trapezoidal shape and were very low. The heating apparatus and chimney were at opposite ends of the furnace, so that it was equally heated over its entire length. These furnaces, made of firebrick, consisted simply of a grate for burning the coal and a hearth on which the iron bars were laid. This hearth, inclined at an angle of twenty-five degrees, enabled the molten metal to flow into troughs from which 1,200 converging gutters would take it to the central shaft.

The day after the boring and building operations had been completed, Barbicane gave orders to begin work on the inner mould. A cylinder nine hundred feet high and nine feet across had to be placed inside the shaft so that it would exactly fill

---

[1] It is by removing this carbon and silicon by the refining process in a puddling furnace that cast-iron is transformed into ductile iron.

the space reserved for the bore of the Columbiad. This cylinder was composed of a mixture of clayey earth and sand to which hay and straw had been added. The space left between the mould and the masonry was to be filled by the molten metal, which would thus form walls six feet thick.

To hold this cylinder upright, it had to be strengthened with iron reinforcements and steadied at regular intervals by cross-pieces fixed in the stone revetment. After the casting these cross-pieces would be buried inside the metal and would have no harmful effect on it.

This operation was completed on 8th July and the casting was scheduled for the next day.

'This casting festival will be a beautiful ceremony!' said J. T. Maston to his friend Barbicane.

'No doubt,' replied Barbicane, 'but it won't be a public ceremony.'

'What, you aren't going to open the enclosure to all comers?'

'Of course not, Maston. Casting the Columbiad will be a delicate, not to say dangerous, operation, and I prefer to have it done behind closed doors. Once the projectile has been fired, you can have a festival if you want, but not till then.'

The president was right, the operation might offer un-expected dangers, and a large crowd of onlookers might make it impossible to take effective counter-measures. The workers had to keep their freedom of movement. No one, therefore, was allowed inside the enclosure, except for a delegation of members of the Gun Club who had made the trip to Tampa. They included the dashing Bilsby, Tom Hunter, Colonel Blomsberry, Major Elphiston, General Morgan and others for whom the casting of the Columbiad was a matter of personal interest. J. T. Maston appointed himself their guide. He spared them no detail; he took them everywhere—to the powder magazines, the workshops, the machines—and he made them inspect the 1,200 furnaces one after another. By the time they had made their 1,200th inspection their enthusiasm had worn off a little.

The casting was to take place on the stroke of noon. The day before, each furnace had been loaded with 114,000 pounds of metal in bars, arranged in crossed piles so that the hot air could circulate freely among them. The 1,200 chimneys had been spewing their torrents of flame into the air since morning, while the ground was shaken by dull tremors. For each pound of metal to be melted a pound of coal had to be burned, so 68,000 tons of coal sent up a thick curtain of black smoke before the sun.

The heat soon became unbearable inside this circle of furnaces, whose roaring was like the rumble of thunder. Powerful blowers added the noise of their blast as they saturated the glowing furnaces with oxygen.

To succeed, this operation had to be carried out rapidly. At the signal given by the firing of a cannon, each furnace was to release its quota of molten metal and empty itself completely.

When all the preparations had been made, the workers and foremen waited for the signal with impatience mingled with a certain excitement. There was no one in the enclosure now, and each casting foreman was at his post beside the tapholes.

Barbicane and his colleagues watched the operation from a nearby knoll. In front of them was a cannon ready to be fired at a sign from the engineer.

A few minutes before noon, the first drops of metal began to flow. The troughs gradually filled, and when the metal was entirely liquid it was kept in abeyance for a few moments, in order to facilitate the separation of foreign substances.

Twelve o'clock struck. The cannon fired, throwing its tawny lightning into the air. Twelve hundred tapholes opened at once, and 1,200 snakes of fire crawled towards the central shaft, unrolling their incandescent coils. There, with a fearful din, they plunged to a depth of nine hundred feet. It was a moving and magnificent spectacle. The ground trembled while these waves of molten iron, sending whirlwinds of smoke towards the sky, volatilized the moisture in the mould and shot it through the vent-holes in the stone revetment, in the form of dense vapour. These artificial clouds spiralled up to a height of 3,000 feet. An Indian wandering beyond the horizon might have imagined that a new volcano was being formed in the heart of

Florida, but this was not an eruption, a tornado, a storm, a struggle of the elements, or any of the other terrifying phenomena which Nature is capable of producing. No, it was man alone who had created these reddish vapours, these gigantic flames worthy of a volcano, these loud tremors like the convulsions of an earthquake, this roar which could rival any hurricane or tempest, and it was his hand which had precipitated, into an abyss which he himself had dug, a whole Niagara of molten metal.

16

The Columbiad

HAD the casting operation been successful? Everyone was reduced to mere conjecture. There was every reason to believe that it had been successful, however, since the mould had absorbed the entire mass of metal which had been melted in the furnaces. But whatever the truth of the matter, it would be impossible to make any direct check for a long time.

When Major Rodman cast his 160,000-pound cannon the cooling process took no less than fifteen days. How long, then, was the monstrous Columbiad, wreathed in swirls of vapour and defended by its intense heat, going to be hidden from its admirers' gaze? It was difficult to calculate.

During this time the patience of the Gun Club members was put to a severe test. But there was nothing to be done about it. J. T. Maston's devotion nearly led to his being roasted alive. Two weeks after the casting, a huge plume of smoke was still rising into the sky and the ground was too hot to stand on within a radius of two hundred yards around the top of Stone Hill.

The days went by, the weeks followed one another. There was no way of cooling the immense cylinder. It was impossible to go near it. There was nothing to do but wait, and the members of the Gun Club fretted impatiently.

'It's already 10th August!' J. T. Maston said one morning. 'Less than four months till December! And we still have to take out the core, tertiate the bore of the Columbiad, and load it! We won't be ready! We can't even go near the cannon! Isn't it ever going to cool? What a cruel joke it would be if it never cooled down!'

The impatient secretary's friends tried to calm him, though in vain. Barbicane said nothing, but his silence concealed an inner irritation. To find himself stopped by an obstacle which could be surmounted only by time, a formidable enemy in the circumstances, and to be completely at the mercy of an adversary was a hard thing for an old soldier to endure.

Daily observations finally revealed a certain change in the state of the ground. By 15th August the rising vapours had diminished noticeably in intensity and thickness. A few days later the ground was exhaling only a light mist, the last breath of the monster enclosed in its stone coffin. Little by little the tremors of the ground died down and the circle of heat shrank. The more impatient onlookers moved closer. One day they gained ten feet, the next day twenty. On 22nd August Barbicane, the other members of the Gun Club and the engineer were able to stand on the sheet of iron at the top of Stone Hill. It was certainly a healthy place, for it was impossible to have cold feet there.

'At last!' cried the president of the Gun Club with a great sigh of satisfaction.

Work was resumed that same day. They at once proceeded to take out the inner mould in order to free the bore of the cannon. Picks, mattocks and drilling equipment were used day and night. The clayey earth and sand had been made extremely hard by the heat, but with the aid of machines, the workers overcame this mixture, which was still hot from contact with the cast-iron walls of the cannon. The material removed was rapidly taken away in steam-driven wagons. The men worked so hard and enthusiastically, Barbicane urged them on so earnestly, and his arguments were presented with such force, in the shape of dollars, that by 3rd September all traces of the mould had disappeared.

The operation of boring was immediately begun. The machines were installed without delay, and swiftly worked powerful borers whose cutting edges bit into the rough surface of the cast-iron. A few weeks later the inner surface of the immense tube was perfectly cylindrical and the bore of the cannon had acquired a thorough polish.

Finally, on 22nd September, less than a year after Barbicane's announcement, the huge cannon's verticality and bore were carefully checked by delicate instruments and it was pronounced ready for action. There was nothing to do now but wait for the moon, and everyone was sure it would keep its appointment.

J. T. Maston's joy knew no bounds. He nearly had a terrible fall when he looked down into the nine-hundred-foot tube. If it had not been for Blomsberry's right arm, which the worthy colonel had fortunately kept, Maston, like a latter-day Erostratus, would have met his death in the depths of the Columbiad.

The cannon was finished. There could no longer be any possible doubt that it would turn out perfectly; so on 6th October Captain Nicholl reluctantly paid his bet and President Barbicane entered the sum of two thousand dollars in his books. There is every reason to believe that the captain was so angry he actually fell ill. However, he still had three bets of three, four and five thousand dollars, and if he could win two of them he would still come out of the affair quite well. But money was not his chief concern; his rival's success in casting a cannon which not even fifty-foot armour-plating could have withstood was a terrible blow to him.

Since 23rd September the enclosure on Stone Hill had been open to the public, and it is not difficult to imagine what crowds came flocking in.

Swarms of people from all over the United States converged on Florida. The town of Tampa had grown enormously during the year it had devoted entirely to the work of the Gun Club, and it now had a population of 150,000. After swallowing up Fort Brooke in a maze of streets, it now stretched out onto the tongue of land which divides Espiritu Santo Bay into two parts. New districts, new squares and a whole forest of houses had sprung up on those formerly deserted shores, in the heat of the American sun. Companies had been formed for the construction of churches, schools and private dwellings, and in less than a year the area of the town increased tenfold.

It is well known that the Yankees are born business men; wherever fate leads them, from the tropics to the icy north, their business instinct must find some useful outlet. That is why people who had come to Florida simply out of curiosity, to watch the operations of the Gun Club, allowed themselves to be drawn into business ventures as soon as they had settled down in Tampa. The ships which had been chartered for transporting workers and material had made the port busier than it had ever been before. Soon other ships, of all shapes and sizes, laden with food, supplies and merchandise, criss-crossed the bay and the two roadsteads. Shipowners and brokers set up large offices in the town, and every day the *Shipping Gazette* reported new arrivals in the port of Tampa.

Roads multiplied around the town and, in view of the enormous growth of its population and business, it was finally connected by rail with the southern states of the Union. A railway linked Mobile and Pensacola, the great southern naval arsenal; then, from this important point, it went on to Talla-hassee. There it met a small section of track, twenty-one miles long, by which Talahassee was already connected with Saint Marks on the coast. This strip of railway was extended to Tampa, and on its way it revived and awakened the dead or sleeping parts of central Florida. Thus Tampa, thanks to those wonders industry derived from an idea which had hatched in a man's brain one fine day, earned the right to assume the airs of a big city. It had been nicknamed ' Moon City ', and the capital of Florida went into a total eclipse, visible from all over the world.

It will now be easy to understand why the rivalry between Texas and Florida was so great, and why the Texans were so angry when their claims were dismissed by the Gun Club's choice. In their far-sighted wisdom they had realized how much a region could gain from Barbicane's project, and the benefits which would accompany such a mighty cannon shot. Texas had lost a great business centre, railways and a considerable

H

growth in population. All these advantages had gone to that wretched Florida peninsula, lying like a breakwater between the waves of the Gulf of Mexico and the breakers of the Atlantic. Barbicane was therefore no more popular in Texas than General Santa Anna.

Meanwhile, despite its commercial ardour and its industrial frenzy, Tampa was far from forgetting the Gun Club's fascinating operations. On the contrary, its inhabitants took an excited interest in the smallest details of the project and in every stroke of the pick. There was constant travel to and fro between the town and Stone Hill; it was a veritable procession, or, better still, a pilgrimage.

It was already clear that on the day of the experiment the spectators would be numbered in millions, for they were already gathering on the narrow peninsula from all over the world. Europe was emigrating to America.

But it must be admitted that so far the curiosity of these countless newcomers had been poorly satisfied. Many of them had counted on seeing the spectacle of the casting, and had seen only its smoke. That was very little for avid eyes, but Barbicane had refused to let anyone watch the operation. The result was grumbling, dissatisfaction and complaining. The president was fiercely criticized; he was accused of despotism; his conduct was described as un-American. There was almost a riot around the stockade at Stone Hill. Barbicane, as we have seen, remained utterly inflexible.

But when the Columbiad had been completely finished the closed-door policy could no longer be maintained. It would have been ungracious, and even imprudent, to irritate public feeling. So Barbicane opened his enclosure to all comers. However, prompted by his practical mind, he decided to make money out of the public's curiosity.

It was a great experience simply to look at the huge Columbiad, but to descend into its depths was something that every American regarded as the *ne plus ultra* of earthly bliss. There was not one visitor who did not want to have the pleasure of seeing that abyss of metal from the inside. Platforms suspended from a steam winch enabled them to satisfy their curiosity. The idea was a huge success. Women, children, old people, everyone felt in duty bound to plumb the mysterious depths of the colossal cannon. The price for the descent was five dollars per person, which was by no means cheap, yet during the two months preceding the experiment the rush of visitors enabled the Gun Club to put half a million dollars into its treasury.

Needless to say, the first men to visit the interior of the Columbiad were the members of the Gun Club, enjoying an honour to which that illustrious organization was fully entitled. The solemn ceremony took place on 25th September. A cage of honour lowered President Barbicane, J. T. Maston, Major Elphiston, General Morgan, Colonel Blomsberry, the engineer Murchison and other distinguished members of the famous club. There were ten of them in all. It was still quite hot at the bottom of that long metal tube, and they all suffocated a little. But what joy! What bliss! A table set for ten had been placed on the massive stone which supported the Columbiad, whose interior was brightly illuminated by a beam of electric light. Numerous exquisite dishes, which seemed to descend from the sky, were successively placed before the guests, and the finest French wines flowed in profusion during that magnificent meal served nine hundred feet underground.

The banquet was very lively and even very noisy. Toasts were proposed right and left. The guests drank to the earth, the Gun Club, the United States, the moon, Phoebe, Diana, Selene, the Queen of the Night and the 'peaceful courier of the firmament'. All those cheers, borne on the sound waves of the huge acoustic tube, reached its upper end like thunder, and the crowd gathered around Stone Hill cheered in reply, joining in spirit the ten guests at the bottom of the gigantic Columbiad.

J. T. Maston was beside himself with joy. It would be difficult to say whether he shouted more than he gesticulated, or whether he drank more than he ate. In any case, he would not have given up his place for an empire—not even, he said, if the cannon were already loaded and primed and about to be fired, sending him into interplanetary space in little pieces.

17

A cablegram

THE great task undertaken by the Gun Club was to all intents and purposes finished, yet two months still had to go by before the day when the projectile would set off for the moon. Because of the impatience felt by the whole world, those two months were going to seem as long as two years. So far the newspapers had reported the smallest details of the operation, and these had been eagerly devoured; but now it seemed likely that this 'dividend of interest' distributed to the public was going to be seriously diminished, and everyone was afraid of no longer being able to obtain his daily ration of excitement.

These fears proved to be unfounded. The most unexpected, extraordinary, incredible incident raised interest to a fever pitch again and threw the whole world once more into a state of violent agitation.

On 30th September, at 3.47 p.m., a dispatch which had been sent by means of the Atlantic cable which runs along the ocean bed from Valencia in Ireland to Newfoundland and the American coast was delivered to President Barbicane.

He opened the envelope and read the dispatch. In spite of his great self-control, when he read the short message in the cablegram his lips turned pale and his eyes became blurred.

Here is the text of that cablegram, which is now preserved in the archives of the Gun Club:

> PARIS, FRANCE, 30 SEPTEMBER 04.00
> BARBICANE
> TAMPA, FLORIDA, U.S.A.
>
> REPLACE SPHERICAL SHELL WITH CYLINDRO-CON-ICAL PROJECTILE. WILL GO TO THE MOON IN IT. AM COMING ON STEAMER *ATLANTA*.
>
> MICHEL ARDAN

18

The passenger on the *Atlanta*

IF, INSTEAD of flashing along electric wires, this astounding message had arrived simply by post and in a sealed envelope, so that a series of French, Irish, Newfoundland and American clerks were not necessarily aware of its contents, Barbicane would not have hesitated for a moment. He would have remained silent out of prudence and in order not to discredit his project. This cablegram might be a hoax, especially coming as it did from a Frenchman. What likelihood was there that any man could be bold enough even to consider such a trip? And if such a man existed, was he not a madman who ought to be put in a padded cell rather than in a projectile?

But the contents of the cablegram were known, for telegraph services are not very discreet by nature, and the news of Michel Ardan's proposal was already spreading across the whole Union. It was therefore pointless for Barbicane to remain silent. He called together those of his colleagues who were in Tampa and, without revealing his thoughts or discussing the amount of credence which should be given to the cablegram, he coldly read out its laconic text.

'Impossible!'

'Incredible!'

'It must be a joke!'

'He's making fun of us!'

'Ridiculous!'

'Absurd!'

For several minutes the company gave vent to every variety of expression of doubt, incredulity and derision, accompanied by the gestures which are customary in such cases. Each man smiled, laughed or shrugged his shoulders, according to his mood. Only J. T. Maston produced a superb response:

'Now *that*'s an idea!' he cried.

'Yes,' said the Major, 'but if it's all right to have ideas like that, it's only on condition that you have no intention of carrying them out.'

'Why not?' the secretary of the Gun Club replied hotly, ready to argue. But nobody tried to push him any further.

Meanwhile the name of Michel Ardan was already being repeated in Tampa. Strangers and natives exchanged looks, questioned one another and made jokes, not about that European, who was only a myth, an invention, but about J. T. Maston for believing in the existence of that legendary individual. When Barbicane had proposed sending a projectile to the moon, everyone had considered that a natural and practical undertaking, simply a matter of ballistics. But that a sane man should offer to travel in the projectile, to attempt that fantastic journey—that was a whimsical idea, a joke, a hoax, or, to use a word common to both Frenchmen and Americans, *humbug!*

The jokes went on till evening without stopping. It can be said that the whole Union was seized with a fit of uncontrollable laughter, which is unusual in a country where impossible undertakings readily find advocates, supporters and backers.

However, like all new ideas, Michel Ardan's proposal irritated certain minds. It disturbed the course of normal emotions. It was something nobody had thought of before. The incident soon became an obsession because of its very strangeness. People kept thinking about it. How many things have been denied one day, only to become realities the next! Why shouldn't someone travel to the moon some day? But in in any case the man who wanted to risk his life that way must be a madman, and since his plan could not be taken seriously, he would have done better to keep quiet, instead of upsetting a whole country with his ridiculous nonsense.

But first of all, did the man really exist? It was an important question. The name of Michel Ardan was not unknown in America. It belonged to a European who was often cited for his daring feats. Besides, this cablegram sent across the bottom of the Atlantic, the naming of the ship on which the Frenchman had said he was travelling, the date set for his arrival—all these factors lent the proposal a certain plausibility. The matter had to be cleared up soon. Isolated individuals formed into groups, the groups were drawn together by curiosity like atoms by molecular attraction, and the final result was a compact crowd which moved towards President Barbicane's residence.

Since the arrival of the telegram, Barbicane had not declared his opinion. He had let J. T. Maston state his views without expressing either approval or disapproval. He lay low, intending to wait on events. But he had reckoned without the impatience of the public, and it was with a certain displeasure that he saw the population of Tampa gathering beneath his windows. Soon murmurs and shouts forced him to appear. He had all the duties and consequently all the vexations of fame.

And so he appeared. Silence fell, until one citizen spoke up and asked bluntly:

'Is the man called Michel Ardan in the cablegram on his way to America or not?'

'Gentlemen,' replied Barbicane, 'I don't know any more about that than you do.'

'We must find out!' shouted some impatient voices.

'Time will tell,' the president replied coldly.

'Time has no right to keep a whole country in suspense,' said the spokesman. 'Have you changed your plans for the projectile, as the cablegram asks?'

'Not yet, gentlemen. But you are right: we must find out. Since the telegraph has caused all this commotion, it should give us more complete information.'

'To the telegraph office!' cried the crowd.

Barbicane went down to the street and made for the telegraph office, followed by the huge assembly.

A few minutes later, a dispatch was on its way to the ship-brokers' office in Liverpool, asking the following questions:

'Is there a ship called the *Atlanta*? When did she leave Europe? Does she have a Frenchman called Michel Ardan on board?'

Two hours later, Barbicane received an answer too exact to leave any room for doubt:

'The steamer *Atlanta*, of Liverpool, put to sea on 2nd October, bound for Tampa, with a Frenchman on board listed under the name of Michel Ardan.'

When he had read this confirmation of the first cablegram, the president's eyes flashed, his fists clenched violently and he was heard to murmur:

'So it's true! It's possible! That Frenchman exists! And in two weeks he'll be here! But he's a madman, a lunatic! I'll never agree . . .'

Yet that very evening he wrote to Breadwill and Co., asking them to postpone casting the projectile until further notice.

To describe the emotion which gripped the whole of America, the way in which the effect of Barbicane's original announce-ment was surpassed a dozen times, what the Union newspapers said, how they accepted the news and trumpeted the arrival of that hero from the Old World, the feverish excitement in which everyone lived, counting the hours, minutes and seconds; to give even a faint idea of the exhausting obsession of all those minds dominated by a single thought; to show all occupations giving place to a single preoccupation, work stopped, business suspended, ships ready to put to sea remaining in port so as not to miss the arrival of the *Atlanta*, trains arriving full and leaving empty, Espiritu Santo Bay constantly criss-crossed by steamers, packet boats, yachts and flyboats of all sizes; to enumerate the thousands of people who quadrupled the popu-lation of Tampa in two weeks and had to camp in tents like an army in the field—all this would be a task beyond human ability, and could not be undertaken without reckless temerity.

On 20th October, at nine o'clock in the morning, the signal stations on the Bahama Channel reported thick smoke on the horizon. Two hours later, a big steamer exchanged signals with them. The name of the *Atlanta* was immediately sent to Tampa. At four o'clock the English ship entered Espiritu Santo Bay. At five she steamed into Hillsboro roadstead at full speed. At six she dropped anchor in Tampa harbour.

Before the anchor had bitten into the sandy bottom, the *Atlanta* was surrounded by five hundred small boats and taken by storm. Barbicane was the first to step on board. He cried out in a voice whose emotion he tried in vain to control:

'Michel Ardan!'

'Present!' replied a man standing on the poop deck.

With folded arms, questioning eyes and sealed lips Barbicane gazed intently at the *Atlanta*'s passenger.

He was a man of forty-two, tall but already a little round-shouldered, like those caryatids which hold balconies on their backs. He had a massive leonine head, and he occasionally shook his red hair, which looked like a positive mane. A short face with a broad forehead, a moustache which bristled like a cat's whiskers, cheeks adorned with little tufts of yellowish hair, and round, rather wild, near-sighted eyes completed that eminently feline physiognomy. But his nose was boldly drawn, his mouth particularly humane, his forehead high, intelligent and furrowed like a field which is never left fallow. Finally, his well-developed torso firmly planted on a pair of long legs, his strong muscular arms, and his resolute bearing made the European a solidly built man, 'forged rather than cast', to borrow a phrase from the metallurgical art.

Disciples of Lavater or Gratiolet would easily have detected on his skull and face the incontestable signs of a combative nature, in other words courage in danger and a tendency to crush obstacles in his path. They would also have seen signs of kindness and a lively imagination, a faculty which leads certain temperaments to incur a passion for superhuman things. On the other hand the bumps of acquisitiveness, the need to possess and acquire, were entirely absent.

To finish describing the physical appearance of the *Atlanta*'s passenger, we must mention his loose, comfortable clothes, his

coat and trousers so generously cut that Michel Ardan nicknamed himself 'Cloth-bane', his loosely tied cravat, his shirt col-
lar wide open on his robust neck, and his invariably unbuttoned
cuffs, from which his restless hands emerged. He gave the impression that, even in the depths of winter or in the midst of danger,
he was never cold, and that he certainly never had cold feet.

On the deck of the steamer, in the midst of the crowd, he
paced up and down, never staying in one place, 'dragging his
anchor', as the sailors said, gesticulating, speaking familiarly
to everyone and biting his nails nervously. He was one of those
eccentrics whom the Creator invents in a moment of whimsy,
breaking the mould immediately afterwards.

Michel Ardan's personality offered great scope for observation and analysis. This astonishing man was perpetually inclined to indulge in exaggeration and had not yet passed the age
of superlatives. Objects were registered on his retina with inor-
dinate dimensions, and this led to an association of gigantic ideas.
He saw everything larger than life, except difficulties and men.

He had a luxuriant nature; he was an artist by instinct, and
a wit who used sniper tactics rather than keeping up a running
fire of amusing remarks. In a discussion he showed little regard
for logic and was hostile to the syllogism, which he would never
have invented, but he had his own methods of attack. A quarrel-
some type, he was a master of the *ad hominem* argument, and he
liked to defend hopeless causes tooth and claw.

Among other idiosyncracies, he declared himself to be 'sub-
limely ignorant', like Shakespeare, and he professed to despise
scholars, who were, he said, 'people who do nothing but keep
the score while we play the game'. He was a Bohemian from
Wonderland, adventurous but not an adventurer, a dare-devil,
a phaethon driving the sun chariot at breakneck speed, an
Icarus with a pair of spare wings. He never shunned danger,
and threw himself into mad ventures with his eyes wide open;
he burned his ships behind him with more enthusiasm than
Agathocles, and, ready to break his neck at any time, he
invariably ended up by falling on his feet, like those little
wooden acrobats children play with.

. . . love of the impossible was his ruling passion

In two words, his motto was 'Why not?' and love of the impossible was his ruling passion, to use Pope's excellent expression.

But he also had the defects that went with his good qualities. Nothing ventured, nothing gained; he ventured often, but had little to show for it. He was a spendthrift, a wastrel. Completely unselfish, he was as soft-hearted as he was headstrong. Obliging and chivalrous, he would not have signed the death warrant of his cruellest enemy, and he would have sold himself into slavery to buy the freedom of a slave.

In France and all over Europe, everyone knew that showy, noisy man. The hundred voices of fame had talked themselves hoarse in his service. He lived in a glass house and confided his most intimate secrets to the whole world. He also had an admirable collection of enemies among those whom he had annoyed, wounded or mercilessly knocked down as he elbowed his way through the crowd.

Generally speaking, however, he was liked and treated as a spoiled child. To quote the popular expression, you had to 'take him or leave him', and people took him. Everyone was interested in his bold ventures and watched him anxiously. He was so reckless and daring! Whenever a friend tried to stop him by predicting imminent disaster, he would smile amiably and answer: 'The forest is burned only by its own trees,' without realizing that he was quoting the prettiest of all Arab proverbs.

Such was the *Atlanta*'s passenger, always agitated, always boiling with the heat of an inner fire, passionately excited, not about what he had come to do in America—he was not even thinking about it—but simply because of his feverish nervous system. If ever two men presented a striking contrast, it was the Frenchman Michel Ardan and the American Barbicane, though each was enterprising, bold and daring after his fashion.

The president's contemplation of this rival who had just thrust him into the background was soon interrupted by the cheers of the crowd. Their shouting became so frenzied, and their enthusiasm took such a personal form, that Michel Ardan, after shaking a thousand hands at the risk of losing all his fingers, had to take refuge in his cabin.

Barbicane followed him without having said a single word.

'You're Barbicane?' Ardan asked him as soon as they were alone together, in the same tone he would have used in speaking to a friend he had known for twenty years.

'Yes.'

'Then how do you do, Barbicane? How are things? Fine? That's good!'

'Are you determined to go through with it?' Barbicane asked without any preliminaries.

'Absolutely determined.'

'Nothing will make you change your mind?'

'Nothing. Have you modified your projectile as I asked you to in my cablegram?'

'I was waiting for you to arrive . . . But tell me,' Barbicane said insistently, 'have you thought it over carefully?'

'Thought it over? I can't waste time doing that. I've found a chance to go on a trip to the moon, I'm going to take it, and that's all there is to it. I don't see why I should think it over.'

Barbicane stared at this man in fascination, who spoke of his proposed journey so lightly and casually, and with such a complete lack of anxiety.

'But you must at least have some plan in mind, some means of carrying out your project?'

'Yes, I have an excellent plan, my dear Barbicane. But if I may say so, I'd rather tell my story once for all, to everyone, and then have done with it. That way I won't have to repeat myself. So, if you have no objections, call together your friends, your colleagues, the whole town, the whole state, the whole country if you like, and tomorrow I'll be ready to describe my plan and answer any objections which may be raised. Don't worry: I'll be waiting for them with complete confidence. Does that suit you?'

'It does,' replied Barbicane.

The president then left the cabin and told the crowd about Michel Ardan's suggestions. His words were received with a stamping of feet and shouts of joy. The next day, everyone would be able to examine the European hero at leisure. Some of the more obstinate sightseers, however, refused to leave the deck of the *Atlanta* and spent the night on board. Among them was J. T. Maston, who had screwed his hook into the poop-rail; it would have taken a capstan to pull him loose.

'He's a hero! A hero!' he shouted again and again. 'We're nothing but a lot of old women compared to that European!'

As for the president, after asking the visitors to leave he went back into the passenger's cabin and stayed there till the ship's bell struck midnight.

Then the two rivals in popularity shook hands warmly and Michel Ardan wished President Barbicane an affectionate good night.

19

A meeting

THE next day the sun rose too late to suit the impatient public. They felt it was behaving lazily for a sun which was to illuminate such a great occasion. Fearing that Michel Ardan might be asked indiscreet questions, Barbicane would have liked to limit his audience to a small number of well-informed people, to his colleagues, for example. It would have been easier to dam up Niagara Falls. He had to give up this idea and let his new friend run the risks of a public appearance. The hall of Tampa's new stock exchange building was judged inadequate despite its colossal size, for the ceremony, for the planned assembly was taking on the proportions of a mass meeting.

The place chosen was a vast plain outside the town. Within a few hours it was sheltered from the rays of the sun : the ships in the harbour, rich in sails, rigging, spare masts and yards, supplied the materials for a gigantic tent. A huge canvas sky soon extended over the baked earth and defended it against the attacks of the sun. Three hundred thousand people assembled under it and braved the stifling heat for several hours, waiting for the Frenchman to arrive. A third of this crowd would see and hear, another third could see little and hear nothing, while the last third could neither see nor hear, although they were no less eager to applaud.

At three o'clock Michel Ardan made his appearance, accompanied by the principal members of the Gun Club.

On his right was President Barbicane, and on his left J. T.
Maston, more radiant than the noonday sun.

Ardan mounted the platform, from which he looked out over
an ocean of black hats. He seemed quite at ease and not at all
embarrassed; he was gay, familiar and amiable, as if he felt
quite at home. He bowed graciously to the cheers which
greeted him. Then, after raising his hand to ask for silence, he
began speaking in perfectly correct English:

'Gentlemen,' he said, 'although it's very hot, I'm going to
take up some of your time to explain a few things about my
plan, which apparently interests you. I'm neither an orator nor
a scientist, and I wasn't expecting to speak in public, but my
friend Barbicane told me it would please you, so I agreed to do
it. Listen to me with your six hundred thousand ears, and please
excuse any mistakes I may make.'

The crowd liked this straightforward beginning, and they
expressed their appreciation with an immense murmur of
satisfaction.

'Gentlemen,' he said, 'you are free to express approval or
disapproval in any way. If that is understood, I'll begin. First
of all, you mustn't forget that you're dealing with an ignorant
man. But his ignorance is so great that he's even ignorant of
difficulties. So it seemed to him a simple, natural, easy matter
to book a passage in a projectile and set off for the moon. It's
a trip which has to be made sooner or later. As for the chosen
means of locomotion, it simply follows the law of progress.
Man began by travelling on all fours, then, one fine day, on
two feet, then in a cart, then in a coach, then in a shandrydan,
then in a stage-coach, then in a railway carriage. Well, the
vehicle of the future is the projectile. The planets themselves
are just projectiles, mere cannon-balls set in motion by the hand
of the Creator. But let's come back to our vehicle. Some of you,
gentlemen, may feel that the speed which will be given to it is
excessive. That isn't true. All the heavenly bodies move faster,
and the earth itself is now carrying us three times as fast in its
motion around the sun. Let me give you a few examples. Only
I ask your permission to express myself in leagues, because I'm

not over-familiar with American measurements, and if I used them I would be afraid of getting my calculations mixed up.'

This request met with no objection, and the speaker went on:

'Here, gentlemen, are the speeds at which the various planets move. I must admit that, despite my ignorance, I know these little astronomical details quite well; but within two minutes you'll be as learned on the subject as I am. Neptune moves at the rate of 5,000 leagues an hour; Uranus at 7,000; Saturn at 8,858; Jupiter at 11,675; Mars at 22,011; Earth at 27,500; Venus at 32,190; and Mercury at 52,520. Some comets have a velocity of 1,400,000 leagues an hour at their perihelion! As for us in our projectile, we'll be dawdling along at a leisurely pace of only 9,900 leagues an hour at the beginning, and our speed will be constantly decreasing! Is that anything to get excited about? Isn't it obvious that all this will be surpassed some day by even greater speeds, whose mechanical agents will probably be light or electricity?'

No one seemed to want to question this assertion by Michel Ardan.

'My dear listeners,' he went on, 'if we are to believe certain narrow-minded people—and narrow-minded is the only word for them—mankind is enclosed in a circle from which there's no escape, and condemned to vegetate on this globe without ever being able to soar into interplanetary space! It's not true! We're about to go to the moon, and some day we'll go to the planets or the stars as easily and quickly and safely as we now go from Liverpool to New York! The oceans of space will soon be crossed like the oceans of the moon. Distance is only a relative term, and it will eventually be reduced to zero.'

Though strongly inclined in favour of the French hero, the crowd was a little taken aback by this bold theory.

Michel Ardan appeared to realize this.

'You don't seem convinced, my dear hosts,' he said with a charming smile. 'Well, let's reason a little. Do you know how long it would take an express train to reach the moon? Three hundred days. That's all. The distance is 86,410 leagues, but what does that amount to? It's less than nine times the circumference of the earth, and there's no sailor or experienced traveller who hasn't covered a greater distance than that in his life. Think of it: my trip will take only ninety-seven hours. You may think that the moon is a long way from the earth and that a man ought to think twice before trying to go there, but what would you say if it were a question of going to Neptune, which moves in an orbit 1,147,000,000 leagues from the sun! There's a trip that not many people could make, even if it cost only ten cents a mile! Baron Rothschild himself, with all his wealth, would be a few million short of having enough to pay his fare, and would have to give up on the way!'

This line of reasoning seemed to please the crowd. What is more, full of his subject, Michel Ardan threw himself into it with superb gusto; feeling that he was being eagerly listened to, he continued with admirable self-assurance:

'Well, my friends, the distance from Neptune to the sun is nothing compared to the distances from here to the stars. Indeed, to express those distances, we must enter that terrifying realm where the smallest numbers have nine digits, and take the billion as our unit. Excuse me for being so well up on this subject, but it's absolutely fascinating. Listen and judge for yourselves. Alpha Centauri is 8,000 billion leagues away; Wega 50,000 billion; Sirius 50,000 billion; Arturus 52,000 billion; Polaris 117,000 billion; Capella 170,000 billion; and other stars are thousands, millions and billions of billions of leagues away! How can anyone so much as mention the wretched little distances which separate the planets from the sun? How can anyone even maintain that they exist? What an error! What a mistake! What an aberration of the senses! Do you know what I think of that system which begins with the sun and ends with Neptune? Would you like to know my theory? It's very simple. In my opinion the solar system is a solid, homogenous body; the planets which compose it press against, touch and adhere to one another, and the space between them is only the space which separates the molecules of the most compact metals, such as silver, iron, gold or platinum. I therefore have a right to maintain, and I say it again with a conviction which I hope to

I

communicate to all of you: "Distance is an empty word; distance does not exist!"'

'Well said! Bravo! Hurrah!' cried the audience with a single voice, electrified by his gestures, his tone and the boldness of his concepts.

'No,' J. T. Maston cried louder than the rest, 'distance doesn't exist!'

Carried away by the violence of his movements and by the impetus of his body, which he was scarcely able to control, he nearly fell off the platform. But he managed to keep his balance, thus avoiding a fall which would have proved to him in brutal fashion that distance was not an empty word. Then the stirring speech continued:

'My friends,' said Michel Ardan, 'I think that question is settled now. If I haven't convinced all of you, it's because I've been timid in my demonstrations and weak in my arguments, and for that you must blame the insufficiency of my theoretical studies. Be that as it may, I repeat that the distance from the earth to its satellite is truly insignificant, unworthy to preoccupy a serious mind. I don't think I'm going too far in saying that in the near future there will be trains of projectiles in which people will be able to travel comfortably from the earth to the moon. There will be no shaking, jolting or derailments to fear, and the passengers will reach their destination rapidly, without fatigue, in a straight line—as the crow flies, to quote your trappers. Within twenty years, half the people on earth will have visited the moon!'

'Hurrah! Hurrah for Michel Ardan!' cried his listeners, even the least convinced.

'Hurrah for Barbicane!' the speaker replied modestly.

This expression of gratitude towards the promoter of the enterprise was greeted with unanimous applause.

'Now, my friends,' Michel Ardan continued, 'if you have any questions to ask me, you'll embarrass a poor man like me, of course, but I'll try to answer them all the same.'

So far the president of the Gun Club had every reason to be satisfied with the direction the discussion had taken. It had dealt with speculative theories, in which Michel Ardan, carried along by his lively imagination, had made a brilliant impression. Barbicane felt he must prevent it from turning to practical matters in which he would probably be much less impressive. He hastened to ask his new friend if he thought the moon or the planets were inhabited.

'You've asked me a big question, Mr President,' the speaker replied, smiling. 'However, if I'm not mistaken, men of great intelligence, such as Plutarch, Swedenborg, Bernardin de Saint-Pierre and many others, have answered it in the affirmative. Looking at it from the point of view of natural history, I'd be inclined to agree with them; I'd tell myself that nothing useless exists in this world, and, answering your question by raising another, my dear Barbicane, I'd say that if those worlds are habitable, they either are, have been or will be inhabited.'

'You're right!' cried the first row of spectators, whose opinion had the force of law for the last ones.

'No one could give a more logical or precise answer,' said the president of the Gun Club. 'The question comes down to this: Are the other worlds habitable? For my part, I believe they are.'

'And I'm certain of it,' said Michel Ardan.

'But there are arguments against the habitability of the other worlds,' said one of the spectators. 'The principles of life would obviously have to be modified on most of them. To take only the planets, it must be either burning hot or fantastically cold on them, depending on how far they are from the sun.'

'I'm sorry I don't know my honourable contradictor personally,' said Michel Ardan, 'because if I did, I'd try to answer him. His objection has a certain validity, but I think that it and all other objections to the habitability of the other worlds can be countered quite successfully. If I were a physicist I'd say that if less heat is set in motion on those planets near the sun, and more on those farther away, that simple phenomenon is enough to balance the temperatures of those worlds, and make them bearable for beings like us. If I were a naturalist, I'd say, like many illustrious scientists, that Nature on our own earth gives us examples of animals living in very different conditions of habitability; fish breathe in a medium which is lethal to other animals; amphibians have a double life which is rather difficult to explain; certain creatures live in the sea at fantastic depths, under pressures of fifty or sixty atmospheres without being crushed; various aquatic insects, insensitive to temperature, are found in springs of boiling water as well as in polar seas; and finally I'd say that we must recognize in Nature a diversity in her means of action which is often incomprehensible but none the less real, and which verges on omnipotence. If I were a chemist, I'd say that meteorites, bodies obviously formed outside our terrestrial world, have shown undeniable traces of carbon, that this substance owes its origin only to living organisms, and that, according to Reichenbach's experiments, it must necessarily have been "animalized". Finally, if I were a theologian, I'd say that, according to Saint Paul, divine redemption seems to have been applied not only to the earth but to all the celestial worlds. But I'm not a theologian, a chemist, a naturalist or a physicist, so in my total ignorance of the great laws which govern the universe, I'll confine myself to this answer: I don't know if the other worlds are inhabited, and since I don't know, I'll go there to find out!'

Did the opponent of Michel Ardan's theories venture any other arguments? It is impossible to say, for the frenzied shouts of the crowd would have prevented any opinion from being heard. When silence had returned to even the farthest groups, the triumphant orator added these final considerations:

'You realize, of course, my good American friends, that I've done no more than scratch the surface of this great question. I didn't come here to give you a lecture or defend a thesis on it. There's a whole series of other arguments in favour of the habitability of the other worlds. I won't mention them. But allow me to stress one point. If someone maintains that the planets are uninhabited, just say in reply: "You may be right, if it can be proved that the earth is the best of all possible worlds. But that isn't the case, no matter what Voltaire's Pangloss may have said. The earth has only one satellite, whereas Jupiter, Uranus, Saturn and Neptune have several in their service, an advantage that isn't to be scorned. But the main thing that makes our globe uncomfortable is the inclination of its axis in relation to its orbit. That's what causes the inequality of our days and nights, and the unfortunate diversity of our seasons. On our wretched spheriod it's always either too hot or too cold. We freeze in winter and suffocate in summer. Ours is the planet of colds, chills and pneumonia, while on the surface of Jupiter, for example, whose axis has little inclination,[1] the inhabitants can enjoy unvarying temperatures. There are zones of perpetual spring, summer, autumn and winter. Each Jovian can choose the climate he likes and spend his whole life in freedom from changes in temperature. You'll have to admit that that's one respect in which Jupiter is superior to the earth, not to mention the fact that its years are twelve years longer! What is more, it's obvious to me that, living in such wonderful conditions, the inhabitants of that fortunate world are superior beings, that their scholars are more scholarly, their artists more artistic, their bad people not so bad, and their good people better. And what does our spheroid lack in order to attain that perfection? Very little! Only an axis less inclined in relation to the plane of its orbit.'"

'Well then,' cried an impetuous voice, 'let's unite our efforts and invent some machines to straighten the earth's axis!'

Thunderous applause greeted this proposal, whose author was and could only have been J. T. Maston. The fiery secretary had probably been led by his engineering instincts to put forward this daring suggestion, but it must be said, for it is true, that many of the spectators backed him with their shouts, and if they had had the fulcrum requested by Archimedes, the Americans would doubtless have constructed a lever capable of moving the earth and straightening its axis. But a fulcrum was precisely what those daring mechanics lacked.

Nevertheless this 'eminently practical' idea was enormously successful. The discussion was suspended for a good quarter of an hour, and for a long time afterwards people all over the United States talked of the proposal forcefully put forward by the secretary of the Gun Club.

[1] The inclination of Jupiter's axis in relation to its orbit is only 3° 5'.

20

Attack and riposte

IT SEEMED that this incident was going to put an end to the discussion. It was the 'last word', and nobody could have thought of a better conclusion. But when the agitation had died down, these words were heard, spoken in a loud, stern voice:

'Now that the speaker has indulged his imagination, will he kindly return to his subject, do less theorizing and discuss the practical side of his expedition?'

All eyes turned to the person who had just spoken. This was a thin, gaunt man, with an energetic face and an American-style beard growing abundantly under his chin. Taking advantage of the various excited shifts which had taken place in the audience, he had gradually made his way to the front row. There, with his arms crossed and his eyes shining boldly, he was staring imperturbably at the hero of the meeting. After putting his request, he fell silent, apparently unaffected by either the thousands of gazes converging on him or the murmur of disapproval stirred up by his words. When no answer was given him, he asked his question again with the same sharp, precise intonation, adding:

'We're here to deal with the moon, not with the earth.'

'You are right, sir,' replied Michel Ardan; 'the discussion has wandered off the subject. Let's come back to the moon.'

'Sir,' said the stranger, 'you claim that our satellite is inhabited. Maybe it is, but one thing is sure: if there are any people up there, they live without breathing, because—I'm telling you this for your own good—there isn't a single molecule of air on the moon's surface.'

When he heard this, Ardan shook his tawny mane; he realized that he was going to have to fight this man on the very heart of the matter. He stared back at him and said:

'So there's no air on the moon! Would you mind telling me who says so?'

'The scientists.'

'Really?'

'Really.'

'Sir,' said Michel Ardan, 'joking aside, I have profound respect for scientists who know, but profound contempt for those who don't.'

'Do you know any who belong to that latter category?'

'Yes. In France there's one who maintains that, "mathe-

All eyes turned to the person who spoke

matically", birds can't fly, and there's another whose theories prove that fish aren't made to live in water.'

'I'm not concerned with them, sir. To support what I'm saying, I could cite names you wouldn't reject.'

'I'd be highly embarrassed if you did, sir, I'm a poor ignorant man who asks nothing better than to learn.'

'Then why do you tackle scientific matters if you haven't studied them?' the stranger asked bluntly.

'Why?' retorted Ardan. 'Because a man is always brave if he's unaware of danger! I know nothing, it's true, but my weakness is precisely what makes my strength.'

'Your weakness goes to the point of madness!' the stranger cried angrily.

'If my madness takes me to the moon,' came the Frenchman's riposte, 'so much the better!'

Barbicane and his colleagues had been scrutinizing this intruder, who was trying so boldly to upset Ardan's plan. None of them knew him, and uncertain about the results of such a frank discussion, the president looked at his new friend with a certain apprehension. The spectators were attentive and seriously concerned, for this argument had drawn their attention to the dangers or perhaps even the impossibilities of the expedition.

'Sir,' Michel Ardan's adversary went on, 'the arguments against the existence of any atmosphere on the moon are numerous and unassailable. I would even be prepared to assert that if the moon ever did have an atmosphere, it must have been drawn away from it by the earth. But I prefer to confront you with undeniable facts.'

'Please do, sir,' Michel Ardan replied gallantly. 'Confront me with as many as you like.'

'As you know,' said the stranger, 'when light rays pass through a medium such as air they are deflected from a straight line; in other words, they undergo refraction. Well, when stars are hidden by the moon, the light from them never shows the slightest deviation or gives the smallest sign of refraction when it passes the moon's edge. This clearly means that the moon has no atmosphere.'

Everyone looked at the Frenchman, for if he granted this point, the consequences would be obvious.

'That's your best argument,' replied Michel Ardan, 'not to say your only one, and a scientist might be at a loss to answer it. For my part, I'll say only that that argument isn't absolutely conclusive because it assumes that the angular diameter of the moon has been perfectly determined, which it hasn't. But let's not dwell on that. Tell me, my dear sir, do you admit the existence of volcanoes on the moon's surface?'

'Extinct ones, yes, active ones, no.'

'But it isn't illogical to assume that those volcanoes were active for a certain period in the past, is it?'

'Of course not, but as they themselves could have supplied the oxygen necessary for combustion, the fact of their eruption doesn't prove the existence of an atmosphere.'

'Then let's go on,' said Michel Ardan, 'and leave that sort of argument in favour of direct observation. But I warn you that I'm going to mention names.'

'Mention them.'

'I will. In 1715, when the astronomers Louville and Halley were observing the eclipse of 3rd May, they noticed some strange rapid flashes of light which were frequently repeated. They attributed them to storms raging in the moon's atmosphere.'

'In 1715,' retorted the stranger, 'the astronomers Louville and Halley mistook purely terrestrial phenomena taking place in the earth's atmosphere, such as meteorites, for lunar phenomena. That is what other scientists answered when they first made their announcement, and I make the same answer.'

'Let's go on,' said Ardan, undisturbed by this reply. 'Isn't it true that in 1787 Herschel observed a great many points of light on the surface of the moon?'

'Yes, but he couldn't account for them and he didn't conclude that they indicated the existence of a lunar atmosphere.'

'That was a good answer,' said Michel Ardan, complimenting his adversary. 'I see that you are very knowledgeable on the subject of the moon.'

'Yes, I am, and I'll add that the most expert observers, those who have studied the moon more than anyone else, namely Beer and Mädler, agree that there is no air whatever on its surface.'

The crowd stirred, apparently impressed by the stranger's arguments.

'Let's go on,' said Michel Ardan, 'and we'll come to an important fact. When he was observing the solar eclipse of 18th July 1860, Laussedat, an expert French astronomer, noted that the points of the sun's crescent were rounded and blunted, a phenomenon which could have been produced only by a deviation of the sun's rays passing through the moon's atmosphere, and there can be no other possible explanation.'

'But is the fact certain?' the stranger asked sharply.

'Absolutely certain!'

The crowd stirred again, this time with a renewal of confidence in its hero. His adversary remained silent. Without gloating over his latest advantage, Ardan said simply:

'You can see, my dear sir, that it's unwise to deny the existence of an atmosphere on the moon. It's probably somewhat rarefied, but nowadays science generally admits that it exists.'

'Not on the mountains, with all respect,' retorted the stranger, reluctant to admit defeat.

'No, but it exists in the valleys, even if it doesn't go higher than a few hundred feet.'

'In any case, you'd do well to take precautions, because that air will be terribly thin.'

'Oh, there's sure to be enough for one man! Besides, once I'm up there I'll try to economize as best I can by breathing only on great occasions.'

A huge burst of laughter thundered in the mysterious stranger's ears. He looked round the crowd with proud defiance.

'Since we agree on the existence of a certain amount of air,' Michel Ardan went on nonchalantly, 'we are forced to admit the existence of a certain amount of water. That's a conclusion I'm glad to draw for my own sake. And let me point out something else to my good friend the contradictor: we know only one side of the moon, and while there's probably not much air on the side facing us, it's possible that there's a lot on the other side.'

'Why?'

'Because under the pull of the earth's gravity the moon has taken on the shape of an egg with its small end towards us. This means, according to Hansen's calculations, that its centre of gravity is in the other hemisphere: so we can conclude that all its air and water must have been drawn to the other side of our satellite in the first days of its creation.'

'Pure fantasy!' cried the stranger.

'No, pure theory based on the laws of mechanics, and I think it would be hard to refute it. I appeal to this assembly. Let's put the question to the vote: Is life, as it exists on earth, possible on the surface of the moon?'

Three hundred thousand people shouted a single affirmative. Michel Ardan's adversary tried to speak, but was unable to make himself heard any longer. He was deluged with shouts and threats.

'Enough! Enough!' cried some.

'Get out!' shouted others.

'Throw him out!' yelled the angry crowd.

But, clinging stubbornly to the platform, he stood his ground and let the storm pass. It would have taken on alarming proportions if Michel Ardan had not quelled it with a gesture. He was too chivalrous to abandon his adversary in such a plight.

'Would you like to add a few words?' he asked graciously.

'Yes, a hundred, a thousand!' the stranger replied heatedly. 'Or rather, no, only a few. If you persist in your plan, you must be . . .'

'Imprudent? How can you call me that when I've asked my friend Barbicane for a cylindro-conical shell so that I won't spin round like a squirrel in a cage?'

'But you poor wretch, the terrible jolt will smash you to pieces as soon as you start!'

'My dear contradictor, you've just put your finger on the

only real difficulty! However, I have too good an opinion of the industrial genius of the Americans to think that they won't overcome it!'

'But what about the heat developed by the projectile as it passes through the layers of air?'

'It's walls are thick, and I'll take so little time to get through the earth's atmosphere!'

'What about food and water?'

'I've calculated that I can take along enough for a year, and my journey will last only four days!'

'But what about air to breathe on the way?'

'I'll make it by chemical processes.'

'And your fall on the moon, assuming you get there?'

'It will only be a sixth as fast as a fall on the earth, since the pull of gravity is only a sixth as strong on the surface of the moon.'

'But it will still be enough to shatter you like a piece of glass!'

'And what's to stop me from slowing down my fall by firing off suitably placed rockets at the right time?'

'All right, suppose all these difficulties are solved, all these obstacles are overcome, all the chances turn out in your favour, and you arrive safe and sound on the moon. How will you get back?'

'I won't.'

At this reply, sublime in its simplicity, the crowd remained silent. But its silence was more eloquent than any shouts of enthusiasm would have been. The stranger took advantage of it to make a final protest.

'You're sure to be killed,' he cried, 'and your senseless death won't even have served science!'

'Go on, my unknown well-wisher: continue with your pleasant predictions!'

'This is too much!' cried Michel Ardan's adversary. 'I don't know why I go on with such a frivolous discussion! Persist in your insane plan if you want to! You're not the one who's to blame!'

'Oh, don't spare my feelings!'

'No, another man will bear the responsibility of your acts!'

'And who is that?' Michel Ardan asked imperiously.

'The ignoramus who organized this whole absurd, impossible project!'

This was a direct attack. Ever since the stranger's intervention, Barbicane had been making violent efforts to control himself and 'burn his smoke', like certain boiler furnaces, but when he heard this insulting reference to himself, he leapt to his feet. He was about to walk over to the adversary who was staring defiantly at him when he was abruptly separated from him.

The platform was suddenly picked up by a hundred stout arms and the president of the Gun Club had to share the honours of triumph with Michel Ardan. The platform was heavy, but nobody had to carry it for long, because each man was arguing, struggling and fighting for the privilege of giving this demonstration the support of his shoulders.

Meanwhile the stranger had not taken advantage of the tumult to leave. Would he have been able to, in fact, in that dense crowd? Probably not. In any case, he stood in the front row, his arms folded, looking intently at President Barbicane.

The latter never lost sight of him. The two men's gazes remained locked together like two quivering swords.

The shouting of the vast crowd continued unabated throughout that triumphal march. Michel Ardan was obviously enjoying it. His face was radiant. Occasionally the platform seemed to pitch and toss like a ship in a storm, but the two heroes of the meeting had their sea legs; they never faltered, and their ship reached port safely in Tampa.

Michel Ardan was lucky enough to manage to escape the last admirers. He fled to the Franklin Hotel, hurried up to his room, and quickly slipped into bed, while an army of a hundred thousand men kept watch under his windows.

During this time a brief, solemn, decisive scene took place between the mysterious stranger and the president of the Gun Club.

Free at last, Barbicane went straight up to his adversary.

'Come,' he said curtly.

The stranger followed him onto the quayside, and they were soon alone at the entrance to a wharf overlooking Jones Fall. There the two enemies looked at each other.

'Who are you?' asked Barbicane.

'Captain Nicholl.'

'I thought so. Till now our paths hadn't crossed . . .'

'So I deliberately crossed yours!'

'You've insulted me!'

'Publicly!'

'And you're going to give me satisfaction for that insult.'

'Straight away.'

'No. I want everything to take place secretly between us. There's a wood known as Skersnaw Wood, three miles outside Tampa. Do you know where it is?'

'Yes.'

'Are you willing to walk into it from one side tomorrow morning at five o'clock?'

'Yes, if you'll walk into it from the other side at the same time.'

'And you won't forget to bring your rifle, will you?' asked Barbicane.

'No, just as I'm sure you won't forget to bring yours,' replied Nicholl.

With these coldly spoken words, the president of the Gun Club and Captain Nicholl parted. Barbicane went home, but instead of getting a few hours' sleep, he spent the night trying to think of a way of softening the initial jolt inside the projectile and solving this difficult problem raised by Michel Ardan during the discussion at the meeting.

2 1

How a Frenchman settles a quarrel

WHILE the conditions of this duel—a terrible, savage kind of duel in which each adversary becomes a man-hunter—were being discussed by the president and the captain, Michel Ardan was resting from the fatigue of his triumph. Though 'resting' is scarcely the right word in this context, for American beds can rival any marble or granite table for hardness.

Ardan was therefore sleeping rather badly, tossing and turning between the napkins which served as his sheets, and he was thinking of installing a more comfortable bunk in his projectile when a loud noise awakened him. His door was being shaken by wild blows, apparently struck with some sort of metal instrument. Loud shouts were mingled with this early morning uproar.

'Open your door!' shouted a voice. 'In the name of heaven, open your door!'

Ardan had no reason to grant such a noisily stated request. However, he got up and opened the door just as it was about to yield to the efforts of his determined visitor.

The secretary of the Gun Club burst into the room. A bombshell could not have entered with less ceremony.

'Last night,' J. T. Maston cried abruptly, 'our president was publicly insulted at the meeting. He challenged his adversary, who is none other than Captain Nicholl! They're fighting this morning in Skersnaw Wood! I learned all this from Barbicane himself. If he is killed, it will mean the end of our project. So this duel must be stopped! There's only one man with enough influence over Barbicane to stop him, and that man is Michel Ardan!'

The secretary of the Gun Club burst into the room

While J. T. Maston was speaking, Michel Ardan, giving up all hope of interrupting him, had quickly pulled on his baggy trousers. Less than two minutes later, the two men were hurrying towards the outskirts of Tampa.

On the way J. T. Maston told Ardan the details of the situation. He explained the real causes of the enmity between Barbicane and Nicholl, how it had existed for many years, and why so far, thanks to mutual friends, the president and the

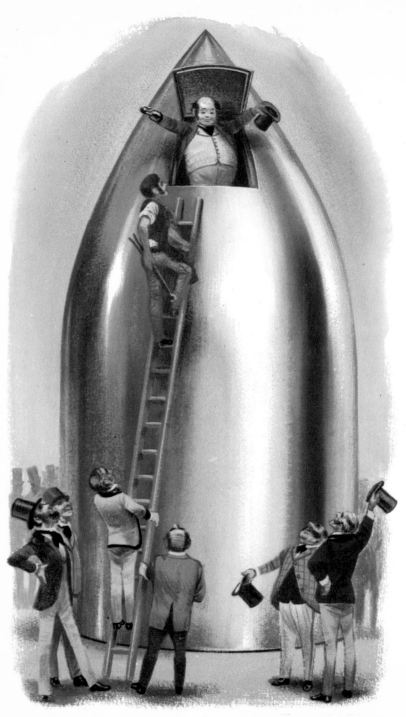

Soon the secretary of the Gun Club appeared at the top of the cone in a triumphant pose. He had put on weight!

captain had never met face to face. He added that it was entirely a matter of rivalry between armour-plating and projectiles, and that the scene at the meeting had simply been an opportunity to work off an old grudge, which Nicholl had been seeking for a long time.

Nothing could be more terrible than these duels peculiar to America, in which each adversary looks for the other in a wood, lies in wait for him in a copse, and tries to shoot him down like an animal in a thicket. Each of them must envy the wonderful qualities so natural to the Indians: their quick intelligence, their immense cunning, their tracking skill, their ability to sense the presence of an enemy. One mistake, one hesitation, one false step can bring death. During these duels the Americans are often accompanied by their dogs, and, hunters and hunted at the same time, they pursue each other for hours on end.

'What devilish people you are!' Michel Ardan exclaimed when his companion had given him a description of the whole procedure.

'That's how we are,' J. T. Maston replied modestly. 'But let's hurry.'

However, although he and Ardan ran through dewy meadows, crossed rice fields, forded creeks and took every short cut they could, they were not able to reach Skersnaw Wood until half-past five, Barbicane was to have entered it half an hour earlier.

Soon they came across an old woodcutter chopping up trees he had felled. Maston ran up to him, shouting:

'Have you seen a man with a rifle come into the woods? It's Barbicane, the president . . . my best friend!'

The worthy secretary of the Gun Club naïvely assumed that his president was known to everyone in the world. But the woodcutter did not seem to understand.

'A hunter,' said Ardan.

'A hunter? Yes, I've seen a hunter,' the woodcutter replied.

'How long ago?'

'About an hour.'

K

'Too late!' cried Maston.

'And have you heard any shots?' asked Michel Ardan.

'No.'

'Not a single one?'

'Not a single one. Your hunter doesn't seem to be having much luck.'

'What shall we do?' asked Maston.

'Go into the wood, at the risk of getting a bullet that isn't meant for us.'

'Ah,' cried Maston in a voice which left no room for doubt, 'I'd rather have a dozen bullets in my head than one in Barbicane's.'

'Then let's go!' said Ardan, after shaking hands with his companion.

A few seconds later the two friends disappeared into the wood. It was a thick forest made of giant cypresses, sycamores, tulip trees, olive trees, tamarinds, oaks and magnolias. The branches of all these trees were mingled in an inextricable tangle which made it impossible to see very far. Michel Ardan and Maston walked side by side, passing silently through the tall grass, pushing their way through strong creepers, peering into the bushes or branches hidden in the thick, dark foliage, and expecting to hear a rifle shot at every step. They were unable to recognize any of the traces Barbicane must have left on his way through the wood; and they walked like blind men along the almost invisible trails, on which an Indian would have been able to follow an adversary step by step.

After an hour of vain searching, they stopped, full of apprehension.

'It must be all over,' Maston said, discouraged. 'A man like Barbicane wouldn't have tried to trick his enemy, set a trap for him, or used any sort of cunning on him. He's too straightforward, too brave. He must have gone straight ahead, into the teeth of danger, and probably so far from the wood-cutter that the wind carried away the sound of the shot.'

'But surely we would have heard a shot in all the time we've been in the wood!' said Michel Ardan.

'But what if we arrived too late?' Maston said in accents of despair.

Michel Ardan could think of no reply. He and Maston began walking again. Now and then they called either Barbicane or Nicholl, but neither of the two adversaries answered. Joyful flocks of birds, roused by the noise, disappeared between the branches, and a few frightened deer ran off into the thickets.

They searched for another hour. By now they had explored most of the wood. There was no trace of the duellists. They were beginning to doubt what the woodcutter had told them, and Ardan was about to give up the futile search, when all of a sudden Maston stopped.

'Sh!' he said. 'There's someone over there!'

'Someone?'

'Yes, a man. He's not moving. His rifle isn't in his hands. What can he be doing?'

'Can you recognize him?' asked Michel Ardan, whose near-sighted eyes were of little use in such circumstances.

'Yes! He's turning around!' replied Maston.

'Who is it?'

'It's Captain Nicholl!'

'Nicholl!' exclaimed Michel Ardan. He felt his heart miss a beat. If Nicholl was unarmed that must mean he had nothing more to fear from his adversary!

'Let's go over to him,' he said 'and find out what's happened.'

But before he and his companion had taken fifty steps they stopped to examine the captain more attentively. They had expected to see a bloodthirsty man obsessed with the idea of revenge; they were dumbfounded at what they saw.

A narrow-meshed net was stretched between two gigantic tulip trees, and in the middle of it was a little bird with its wings caught, struggling and uttering plaintive cries. This inextricable net had been placed there, not by a human being, but by a venomous spider peculiar to the region, wrth huge legs and a body the size of a pigeon's egg. Just as it was about to seize its prey the hideous creature had had to scuttle away and take refuge in the high branches of one of tulip-trees, because a formidable enemy had appeared.

Captain Nicholl had laid his rifle on the ground, forgetting the dangers of his position, and was now trying to free, as gently as possible, the victim caught in the monstrous spider's web. When he had finished, he released the little bird, which fluttered its wings joyfully and flew away.

Nicholl was tenderly watching it vanish when he heard these words spoken with feeling:

'You're a good man! And a kind man!'

He turned round.

'Michel Ardan! What are you doing here?'

'I've come to shake your hand, Nicholl, and prevent you from either killing Barbicane or being killed by him.'

'Barbicane!' exclaimed the captain. 'I've been looking for him for two hours and I can't find him! Where's he hiding?

'Nicholl,' said Michel Ardan, 'that isn't polite. One must always show respect to one's adversary. Don't worry; if Barbicane is alive we'll find him, especially since, if he hasn't stopped like you to rescue birds in distress, he must be looking for you too. But when we do find him, I assure you there won't be any question of a duel between you.'

'Between President Barbicane and me,' Nicholl replied solemnly, 'there is a rivalry so great that only the death of one of us——'

'Come, come!' said Michel Ardan. 'Good men like you two may hate each other, but you must respect each other. You won't fight.'

'I will, sir!'

'No.'

'Captain,' J. T. Maston said in a voice full of emotion, 'I am the president's closest friend, his *alter ego*. If you really have to kill someone, shoot me: it will be exactly the same thing.'

'Sir,' said Nicholl, convulsively gripping his rifle, 'such jokes——'

'My friend Maston isn't joking,' said Michel Ardan, 'and I can understand his idea of dying for a friend. But you're not going to shoot anyone, because I have such an attractive proposal to make to you two rivals that you'll both be eager to accept it.'

'What is it?' Nicholl asked with obvious incredulity.

'Be patient. I can't tell you what it is unless Barbicane is present too.'

'Then let's find him,' cried the captain.

The three men set off at once. After uncocking his rifle, the captain rested it on his shoulder and walked along with a jerky stride, without saying a word.

For another half-hour the search was fruitless. Maston was seized by an ominous foreboding. He looked sternly at Nicholl, wondering whether the captain might not already have satisfied his vengeance and the unfortunate Barbicane might not be lying lifeless in some bloody thicket with a bullet in his heart. Michel Ardan seemed to have the same idea. They were both looking inquiringly at Captain Nicholl when Maston suddenly stopped.

Twenty paces away they saw the motionless head and shoulders of a man sitting with his back against a gigantic catalpa tree half hidden in the grass.

'There he is!' said Maston.

Barbicane did not move. Ardan gazed intently into the captain's eyes, but Nicholl did not flinch. The Frenchman took a few steps and shouted:

'Barbicane! Barbicane!'

No answer. Ardan rushed up to his friend, but just as he was about to grasp his arm he stopped short and uttered an exclamation of surprise.

Barbicane, pencil in hand, was writing formulas and drawing geometrical figures in a notebook. His uncocked rifle lay on the ground.

Engrossed in his work, the scientist had forgotten his duel and his vengeance, and he had neither seen nor heard anything.

But when Michel Ardan put his hand on his, he stood up and stared at him in surprise.

'Ah, it's you!' he cried at last. 'I've found it, my dear fellow, I've found it!'

'You've found what?'

'The means!'

'The means?'

· 'The means of softening the jolt inside the projectile when it's fired.'

'Really?' said Ardan, looking at the captain out of the corner of his eye.

'Yes! It's water, just plain water which will act as a spring . . . Ah, Maston! You too!'

'Yes, it's Maston,' said Michel Ardan, 'and allow me at the same time to introduce Captain Nicholl!'

'Nicholl!' cried Barbicane leaping to his feet. 'I beg your pardon, Captain, I'd forgotten . . . I'm ready . . .'

Michel Ardan intervened before the two enemies had time to challenge each other again.

'Heavens,' he said, 'it's a good thing the two of you didn't meet earlier this morning! We'd be in mourning for one of you now. But, thanks to God, who took a hand in the affair, there's no longer anything to fear. When a man forgets his hatred to immerse himself in problems of mechanics or play tricks on spiders, it means that his hatred isn't dangerous for anyone.'

And he told the president how they had found the captain.

'Now tell me,' he said in conclusion, 'whether two fine men like you were made to shoot holes through each other's heads.'

There was something so unexpected about this rather ridiculous situation that Barbicane and Nicholl did not know what attitude they ought to adopt towards each other. Michel Ardan sensed this, and he decided to hasten their reconciliation.

'My good friends,' he said, putting on his best smile, 'there's never been anything between you but a misunderstanding. Nothing more. To prove that it's all over, and since neither of you is afraid to risk his life, why not accept the proposal I'm about to make to you.'

'Tell us what it is,' said Nicholl.

'Our friend Barbicane believes his projectile will go straight to the moon.'

'I certainly do,' said the president.

'And our friend Nicholl is convinced that it will fall back to earth.'

'I'm sure it will,' said the captain.

'Good!' Ardan went on. 'Now I don't pretend to be able to make you agree with each other, but I will say this to you : Come with me, and we'll see whether we reach our destination or not.'

'What!' exclaimed J. T. Maston in amazement.

On hearing this unexpected suggestion, the two rivals observed each other carefully. Barbicane waited for the captain's answer, Nicholl waited for the president to speak.

'Well?' Ardan said in his most charming tone. 'Why not, seeing that there's no jolt to be afraid of?'

'Done!' cried Barbicane.

But before he had finished uttering this word, Nicholl had uttered it too.

'Hurrah! Bravo! Hip, hip, hooray!' Michel Ardan cried, holding out his hands to the two rivals. 'And now that the matter has been settled, my friends, allow me to treat you in the French manner. Let's go to breakfast!'

22

The new citizen of the United States

THAT day, all America learned at the same time of the duel between Captain Nicholl and President Barbicane and its singular outcome. The part played in this affair by the chivalrous European, his unexpected proposal, which had solved the difficulty, the simultaneous acceptance by the two rivals, the way France and America were going to join together in conquering the moon—everything combined to make Michel Ardan more popular than ever. It is well known what frenzied devotion the Americans can show for an individual. In a country where solemn magistrates harness themselves to a dancer's carriage and pull it in triumph it is easy to imagine the passion aroused by the daring Frenchman. If his horses were not unharnessed, it is probably because he had none, but all the other tokens of enthusiasm were showered on him. There was not one citizen who did not join with him in heart and mind. *Ex pluribus unum*, as the motto of the United States puts it.

From that day on, Michel Ardan never had a moment's rest. He was constantly harassed by deputations from all parts of the Union, and he had to receive them whether he liked it or not. The hands he shook and the people he smiled at were beyond counting. Soon he was exhausted; his voice, hoarsened by innumerable speeches, escaped from his lips only in unintelligible sounds, and he nearly got gastro-enteritis from the toasts he had to drink to every state in the Union. This success would have intoxicated anyone else from the very first day, but Ardan was able to maintain himself in a state of witty and charming semi-inebriation.

Among the deputations of all sorts which assailed him, the 'lunatics' were careful not to forget what they owed to the future conqueror of the moon. One day a few of these poor people, who are quite numerous in America, came to him and asked to be allowed to return to their native land with him. Some of them claimed to be able to speak the lunar language and offered to teach it to him. He good-naturedly indulged their innocent mania and accepted messages to deliver to their friends on the moon.

'A strange madness!' he said to Barbicane after he had sent them away. 'It's a madness which often affects lively minds. One of our most famous scientists, Arago, told me once that many people became highly excited and developed incredible peculiarities every time the moon took possession of them. You don't believe in the influence of the moon on illness, do you?'

'Hardly,' replied the president of the Gun Club.

'I don't believe in it either, yet history has recorded some facts which are surprising to say the least. During an epidemic in 1693, for example, the number of deaths went up on 21st January, when there was an eclipse. The famous Bacon used to faint during eclipses of the moon and didn't recover consciousness until they were completely over. King Charles VI of France had six fits of insanity in 1399, all of them during either the new moon or the full moon. Some doctors have classified epilepsy among illnesses which follow the phases of the moon. Nervous illnesses have often appeared to be influenced by it. Mead tells of a child who went into convulsions whenever the moon went into opposition. Gall noticed that the over-excitement of sickly people increased twice a month, at the time of the new moon and the full moon. And there are countless observations of the same sort about dizzy spells, malignant fevers and somnambulism, all tending to prove that the moon has a mysterious influence on earthly illnesses.'

'But how? Why?' asked Barbicane.

'Why?' said Ardan. 'Well, I'll give you the same answer

that Arago repeated nineteen centuries after Plutarch: "Perhaps it's because it isn't true!"'

In the midst of his triumph Michel Ardan could not escape from any of the ordeals inherent in the position of a famous man. Promoters wanted to exhibit him. Barnum offered him a million dollars to allow him to take him from town to town all over the United States and show him off, like some kind of strange animal. Michel Ardan called him a mahout and sent him off with a flea in his ear.

Although he refused to satisfy the public's curiosity in that way, his portraits, at least, circulated all over the world and occupied the place of honour in every album. They were printed in all formats from life size to the tiny dimensions of a postage stamp. Everyone was able to have his hero in every imaginable pose: head, head and shoulders, full length, full face, profile, three-quarters or from the back. Over a million and a half of them were printed. Ardan had a wonderful opportunity to sell parts of himself as relics, but he did not take advantage of it. If he had wanted to sell his hairs for a dollar apiece he still had enough of them left to make a fortune!

The fact was that this popularity did not displease him. Quite the contrary. He placed himself at the public's disposal and corresponded with people all over the world. His witty remarks were repeated over and over again, particularly those he had never made; many were lent to him, for he was already rich in witticisms, and people lend only to the rich.

There were women among his admirers as well as men, and there were countless 'good matches' he could have made if he had taken it into his head to 'settle down'. Old maids, especially, who had been sitting on the shelf for forty years, dreamed night and day in front of his photographs.

He could easily have found hundreds of female companions, even if he had insisted that they go to the moon with him. Women are either fearless or afraid of everything. But since he had no intention of founding a Franco-American family on the moon, he refused.

'I'm not going up there,' he said, 'to play Adam with a

daughter of Eve! All I'd have to do would be to meet a snake, and then . . .'

As soon as he was finally able to get away from the excessive joys of celebrity, he went with his friends to pay a visit to the Columbiad. He felt he owed it that courtesy at least. Besides, he had become an expert on ballistics since he had begun living with Barbicane, J. T. Maston and their colleagues. His greatest pleasure consisted in telling those worthy artillerymen that they were nothing but charming and skilful murderers. He never tired of making jokes on the subject. When he visited the Columbiad he admired it greatly and went down to the bottom of the gigantic mortar which was soon to send him on his way to the Queen of the Night.

'At least this cannon won't hurt anyone,' he said, 'and that's a rather surprising quality in a cannon. But as for your weapons which destroy, burn, break and kill, don't talk to me about them.'

At this point we must relate an incident involving J. T. Maston. When the secretary of the Gun Club heard Barbicane and Nicholl accept Michel Ardan's suggestion, he resolved to join them and make the group a foursome. One day he asked to be included in the journey. Barbicane, heartbroken at having to turn him down, told him that the projectile could not carry so many passengers. In despair, J. T. Maston went to see Michel Ardan, who told him that he must resign himself, and put forward some *ad hominem* arguments.

'I hope you won't be offended by what I'm going to say, Maston,' he said, 'but between you and me, you're too incomplete to put in an appearance on the moon.'

'Incomplete!' cried the valiant veteran.

'Yes, my good friend. Think what would happen if we met some inhabitants up there. Would you like to give them a deplorable idea of what happens here on earth by letting them see what war is, and showing them that we spend most of our time devouring each other and breaking one another's arms and legs, on a globe which could feed a hundred billion people and now has barely a billion and a quarter? Come, come: you'd make them show us the door!'

'But if you arrive in pieces,' said J. T. Maston, 'you'll be as incomplete as I am!'

'That's true, but we won't arrive in pieces,' replied Michel Ardan.

A preparatory experiment carried out on 18th October had in fact produced excellent results and given grounds for confidence. Wishing to study the effects of the initial jolt inside a projectile, Barbicane had sent for a thirty-two-inch mortar from the arsenal at Pensacola. It was set up on the shore of the Hillsboro roadstead, so that the shell would fall into the sea, for it was a question of testing the jolt on departure and not the impact on arrival.

A hollow shell was carefully prepared for this singular experiment. The inside walls were lined with thick padding over a network of springs made of the finest steel, forming a kind of cotton-wool nest.

'What a shame I can't get into it!' said J. T. Maston, regretting that his size prevented him from taking part in the experiment.

In this charming shell, which could be closed by means of a lid which screwed into place, Barbicane placed first a big cat, and then a squirrel which belonged to the secretary of the Gun Club, and of which he was particularly fond. He wanted to know how this little animal, which was not likely to suffer from dizziness, would be affected by this experimental journey.

The mortar was loaded with 160 pounds of powder and the shell was put in place. Then the weapon was fired.

The projectile promptly shot out of the barrel, majestically described its parabola, reaching a height of about a thousand feet, and descended in a graceful curve to plunge into the water.

A small boat immediately hurried to the spot where it had fallen. Skilled divers leapt into the water and attached cables to the ears of the shell, which was quickly hoisted on board. Less than five minutes had gone by from the time the animals were enclosed to the time when the lid of their prison was unscrewed.

Ardan, Barbicane, Maston and Nicholl were in the boat, and

As soon as the shell was opened, the cat jumped out

they watched the operation with a feeling of interest which can be easily understood. As soon as the shell was opened, the cat jumped out, a little tousled but full of life, and showing no signs of having returned from an aerial expedition. But there was no squirrel. A search was made. Not a trace of him. They had to face the fact: the cat had eaten his travelling companion.

J. T. Maston was greatly saddened by the loss of his poor squirrel, and resolved to pay suitable tribute to the animal as a martyr to science.

After this experiment, all hesitation and fear vanished. In any case, Barbicane's plans were to improve the projectile still more, and almost entirely eliminate the effects of the initial jolt. There was nothing left to do but set off.

Two days later, Michel Ardan received a message from the President of the United States, an honour which he greatly appreciated.

Like his chivalrous compatriot, the Marquis de la Fayette, he had been made an honorary citizen of the United States of America.

23

The projectile coach

AFTER the completion of the famous Columbiad, public interest turned to the projectile, the new vehicle destined to take the three bold adventurers into space. No one had forgotten that in his cablegram of 30th September Michel Ardan had asked for a modification of the plans drawn up by the members of the committee.

At that time President Barbicane had rightly thought that the shape of the projectile was unimportant, for, after going through the earth's atmosphere in a few seconds, it would go the rest of the way in an absolute vacuum. The committee had accordingly agreed on a spherical shape, so that the projectile could spin about and behave as it pleased. But now that it was going to be transformed into a vehicle, it was a different matter. Michel Ardan had no desire to travel like a squirrel in a cage; he wanted to have his head up and his feet down, and to travel with as much dignity as if he were in the basket of a balloon, moving more swiftly of course, but without turning unseemly somersaults.

New plans were sent therefore to Breadwill & Co. in Albany, with instructions to begin work without delay. The redesigned projectile was cast on 2nd November and immediately sent to Stone Hill by means of the eastern railways.

It arrived safely on 10th November; Michel Ardan, Barbicane and Nicholl were impatiently awaiting this 'projectile coach' in which they were going to set off to discover a new world.

It must be said at once that it was a magnificent piece of work, a metallurgical product which did great credit to American industrial genius. It was the first time that aluminium had ever been obtained in such a large mass, and this was rightly regarded as a prodigious feat. The precious projectile sparkled in the sunlight. With its impressive size and its conical cap it might have been taken for one of those thick pepper-box turrets which medieval architects placed at the corners of fortresses. It lacked only loopholes and a weathercock.

'I expect,' said Michel Ardan, 'to see a man at arms come out of it carrying an arquebus and wearing chain mail. We'll be like feudal lords in there, and with a little artillery we'll be able to hold off all the armies of the moon, if there are any.'

'So you like the vehicle?' Barbicane asked his friend.

'Yes, of course,' replied Michel Ardan, who was looking at it with an artist's eye. 'I only regret that it doesn't have a more slender shape and a more graceful cone. It might have had a cluster of engine-turned metal ornaments on the end, with a chimera, for example, or a gargoyle, or a salamander coming out of the fire with outspread wings and open mouth . . .'

'What for?' asked Barbicane, whose practical mind was not very sensitive to the beauties of art.

'What for? Alas, since you ask me the reason, I'm afraid you'll never understand!'

'Tell me, anyway, my good friend.'

'Well, I think we should always put a little art into what we do. It's better that way. Do you know an Indian play called *The Child's Cart*?'

'I've never heard of it,' replied Barbicane.

'I'm not surprised,' said Michel Ardan. 'Well, in that play there's a thief who's about to cut a hole in the wall of a house, but can't decide whether to give it the shape of a lyre, a flower, a bird or an amphora. Now tell me, Barbicane, if you had been a member of the jury, would you have condemned that thief?'

'Without hesitation,' the president of the Gun Club replied, 'especially as he was also guilty of housebreaking.'

An immense jet of flame shot from the bowels of the earth as from a crater

'And I would have acquitted him! That's why you'll never be able to understand me!'

'I won't even try, my valiant artist.'

'But since the outside of our projectile coach leaves something to be desired,' Michel Ardan went on, 'I hope I'll at least be allowed to furnish it as I please, and with all the luxury befitting ambassadors from the earth.'

'As far as the inside in concerned, you can arrange it any way you like!'

But before going on to the aesthetic, the president of the Gun Club had concerned himself with the practical, and the means he had devised for lessening the effects of the initial jolt were applied with perfect precision.

Barbicane had told himself, not without reason, that no spring would be strong enough to deaden the impact, and during his famous stroll in Skersnaw Wood he had finally managed to solve this great difficulty in an ingenious way. He was going to call on water to render him this signal service. Here is how.

The projectile was to be filled with water to a height of three feet, and this water would support a waterproof wooden disk fitting tightly against the inner wall, but able to slide on it. The passengers would be on this circular raft. As for the liquid mass, it would be divided by horizontal partitions which the first shock would break successively. Each layer of water, starting at the bottom, would be driven upwards through pipes, and would thus act as a spring, while the disk, equipped with extremely strong buffers, would not be able to strike the bottom until each of the partitions in turn had been crushed. The passengers would no doubt still experience a violent impact after all the water had been driven out, but the first shock would be almost entirely deadened by this extremely strong spring.

It is true that three feet of water with a surface area of fifty-four square feet would weigh nearly 11,500 pounds, but, according to Barbicane, the force of the gases accumulated in the Columbiad would be enough to overcome this increase in weight; moreover, the water would all be driven out by the jolt in less than a second, and the projectile would then resume its normal weight.

Such was the solution devised by the president of the Gun Club to deal with the serious problem of the initial shock. The work was intelligently understood and capably executed by the engineers of Breadwill and Co. Once the effect had been produced and the water had been driven out, the passengers could easily get rid of the broken partitions and take apart the sliding disk which would support them at the moment of departure.

As for the upper walls of the projectile, they were covered with thick leather padding over coils of fine steel which had the flexibility of watch springs. The pipes through which the water would escape were so completely hidden beneath this padding that it was impossible to suspect their existence.

Thus every imaginable precaution had been taken to deaden the initial jolt, and Michel Ardan remarked that if they let themselves be crushed now, they must be made of very poor material.

The projectile had an outside diameter of nine feet and a height of twelve feet. In order not to exceed the prescribed weight, the thickness of its walls had been reduced a little, and its base, which would have to withstand the thrust of the gases produced by the explosion of the gun-cotton, was reinforced. This in fact is how bombs and cylindro-conical shells are made : their bases are always thicker than their sides.

Entrance into this metal tower was by way of a narrow opening in the side of the cone which looked like the manhole in a steam boiler. It was hermetically closed by means of an aluminium plate, held in place from the inside by strong binding-screws. The passengers would thus be able to leave their mobile prison at will when they reached the moon.

But it was not enough for them to travel to the moon : they had also to be able to see on the way. This was easily arranged. Under the padding there were four portholes with panes of thick optical glass; two in the circular walls of the projectile, a third in its lower part and a fourth in its conical cap. The passengers would thus be able to see the receding earth, the approaching moon and the starry expanses of space. These portholes were protected against the initial shock by solidly embedded plates which could easily be discarded by unscrewing nuts on the inside. In this way, the air in the projectile could not escape, and observation was possible.

All these admirably constructed devices functioned perfectly, and the engineers had shown equal intelligence in fitting out the interior of the projectile.

There were solidly attached containers for the food and water required for the three passengers. The latter could even obtain fire and light by means of gas stored in a special container at a pressure of several atmospheres. They would only have to turn a tap, and this gas would heat and light the comfortable vehicle for six days. It can be seen that nothing was lacking in the way of necessities for life and even comfort. And, thanks to Michel Ardan's artistic instincts, the pleasant was combined with the useful in the form of art objects. He would have turned his projectile into a real artist's studio if he had not been short of space. On the other hand, it would be a mistake to assume that the three passengers were going to be cramped for space in that metal tower. It had an area of fifty-four square feet and a height of about ten feet, enough to give them a certain freedom of movement. They would not have enjoyed such ease in the most comfortable railway coach in the United States.

When the question of food and light had been settled, there remained the question of air. It was obvious that the air in the projectile would not be enough for four days, for in the space of an hour, one man consumes all the oxygen in a hundred litres of air. Barbicane, his two companions and the two dogs he intended to take with him would consume 2,400 litres of oxygen, or about seven pounds, in twenty-four hours. The air in the projectile would therefore have to be renewed. How? By a very simple process, that of Reiset and Regnault, to which Michel Ardan had referred during the discussion at the meeting.

Air is composed, practically speaking, of 21 per cent oxygen and 79 per cent nitrogen. What happens when we breathe? It is a simple phenomenon. We absorb oxygen, which is essential for sustaining life, from the air, and expel the nitrogen intact. Exhaled air has lost nearly 5 per cent of its oxygen and contains an almost equal volume of carbonic acid, that end product of the combustion of the elements of the blood by the inhaled oxygen. In a closed space, therefore, all oxygen in the air is replaced after a certain time by carbonic acid, which is an essentially noxious gas.

The question therefore came down to this: with the nitrogen conserved intact, how could the used oxygen be replenished and how could the carbonic acid be destroyed? It was quite easy, by means of potassium and caustic potash.

Potassium chlorate is a salt which exists in the form of white flakes. When it is heated to a temperature above four hundred degrees centigrade, it turns into potassium chloride, and the oxygen it contains is entirely given off. Now eighteen pounds of potassium chlorate yield seven pounds of oxygen: the amount the passengers needed for twenty-four hours. So much for the problem of replenishing the oxygen.

As for the caustic potash, it has a strong affinity for the carbonic acid mingled in the air. It need only be agitated to make it take over the carbonic acid and form potassium bicarbonate. So much for the problem of absorbing the carbonic acid.

By combining these two processes, it was possible to restore all its life-giving properties to the exhaled air. The two chemists, Reiset and Regnault, had shown this by means of experiments. But it must be admitted that so far the experiment had been performed only on animals. However great its scientific precision, its effect on men was still completely unknown.

These were the facts laid before the meeting at which the important question was considered. Not wishing to leave any doubt about the possibility of living on this artificial air, Michel Ardan offered to try it himself before the departure. But the honour of making this test was energetically demanded by J. T. Maston.

'Since I'm not going with you,' said the worthy artilleryman, 'the least you can do is let me live in the projectile for a week.'

It would have been unkind to refuse him this favour, so his colleagues granted his request. He was given enough food, water, potassium chlorate, and caustic potash for eight days; then on 12th November, at six o'clock in the morning, after shaking hands with his friends and expressly forbidding them to open his prison before six o'clock on the evening of 20th November, he slipped into the projectile and the plate was hermetically closed.

What happened during the eight days? It was impossible to tell. The thickness of the projectile's walls prevented all sounds from reaching the outside.

On 20th November, at exactly six o'clock, the plate was removed from the opening. J. T. Maston's friends were a little worried, but they were promptly reassured when they heard a joyful voice giving a loud cheer.

Soon the secretary of the Gun Club appeared at the top of the cone in a triumphant pose.

He had put on weight!

24

The telescope in the Rocky Mountains

ON 20th October of the previous year, after the closing of the subscription, the president of the Gun Club had turned over to the Cambridge Observatory the money necessary for the construction of a huge telescope. This telescope, whether a refracting or a reflecting instrument, was to be powerful enough to reveal an object of more than nine feet wide on the surface of the moon.

There is an important difference between a refracting and a reflecting telescope; it might be as well to remind readers of it here. A refracting telescope consists of a tube which has at its upper end a convex lens known as the objective, and at its lower end a second lens known as the ocular, to which the observer applies his eye. Light rays from the object pass through the first lens and, by refraction, form an inverted image at its focus.[1] This image is observed through the ocular, which enlarges it just like a magnifying glass. Thus the tube of a refracting telescope is closed at both ends by the objective and the ocular.

The reflecting telescope, on the other hand, is open at its upper end. Light rays from the observed object penetrate it freely and strike a concave, i.e. converging, metal mirror. From there these rays are reflected to a small mirror which sends them to the ocular, which is so arranged as to magnify the image produced.

[1] The focus is the point at which the light rays are reunited after being refracted.

Thus in a refracting telescope it is refraction which plays the principal role, while in a reflecting telescope it is reflection. As a result the former is sometimes simply referred to as a refractor, and the latter as a reflector. The difficulty in making them consists almost entirely in making the objective, whether it be a lens or a metal mirror.

At the time when the Gun Club embarked on its great experiment, these instruments had been brought to a high degree of perfection and gave magnificent results. Science had come a long way since the days when Galileo observed the heavenly bodies with his poor little seven-power refracting telescope.

Since the sixteenth century, telescopes had grown much wider and longer, and had made it possible to probe more deeply into interstellar space than ever before. Among the refracting telescopes in operation at that time were the one at the Pulkovo Observatory in Russia, with a fifteen-inch objective [1]; the one made by the French optician Lerebours, also with a fifteen-inch objective; and the one at the Cambridge Observatory, with a nineteen-inch objective.

Among the reflecting telescopes there were two of remarkable power and gigantic size. The first one, made by Herschel, had a length of thirty-six feet, a mirror with a diameter of four and a half feet, and a magnification of six thousand. The second one was at Birr Castle, in Ireland; it stood in Parsonstown Park and belonged to Lord Rosse. It was forty-eight feet long, its mirror was six feet in diameter,[2] and its magnification was 6,400; an immense stone structure had to be built to house the apparatus

[1] It cost 80,000 roubles.

[2] One often hears of refracting telescopes of much greater length. One of them, with a length of 300 feet, was installed, under Dominique Cassini's direction, at the Paris Observatory. But it should be pointed out that these telescopes had no tube. The objective was suspended in the air by means of masts, and the observer, holding his ocular in his hand, took up his position close to the focus of the objective as possible. It is easy to understand how difficult these instruments were to use, and especially how difficult it was to centre two lenses in such conditions.

required for manœuvring the instrument, which weighed 28,000 pounds.

In spite of these colossal dimensions, however, the magnification obtained never went much beyond six thousand. A magnification of six thousand brings the moon to an apparent distance of thirty-nine miles and makes it possible to see only objects over sixty feet wide, unless they are extremely long.

In order to see Barbicane's projectile, which was nine feet wide and fifteen feet long, the moon had to be brought to an apparent distance of five miles or less, and this would require a magnification of 48,000.

Such was the problem the Gun Club had set the Cambridge Observatory. It would not be stopped by financial difficulties, but the material difficulties remained.

First of all, a choice had to be made between a refractor and a reflector. Refractors have certain advantages over reflectors. With the same objective they make it possible to obtain greater magnification, because light rays passing through the lenses lose less by absorption than by reflection from the metal mirror of a reflector. But there are limits to the thickness which can be given to a lens, for if the lens is too thick, it will not let the light rays pass through it. Moreover, the construction of these huge lenses is difficult and requires a period of years.

Therefore, although the images are illuminated better in a refractor—an immense advantage in observing the moon, whose light is simply reflected—it was decided to use a reflector, which can be made more quickly and permits greater magnification. Since light rays lose a great deal of their intensity in passing through the earth's atmosphere, the Gun Club decided to install the telescope on one of the highest mountains in the country, which would diminish the amount of air which would have to be traversed.

As we have seen, in a reflecting telescope the ocular—that is, the magnifying glass placed before the observer's eye—produces the magnification, and the greater the diameter and focal distance of the objective, the greater the magnification it permits. To obtain a magnification of 48,000, the size of

Herschel's and Lord Rosse's objectives would have to be far surpassed. There lay the difficulty, for the casting of such mirrors is an extremely delicate operation.

Fortunately a few years earlier a scientist at the Institut de France, Léon Foucault, had invented a process which made polishing an objective a simple, speedy matter, by replacing metal mirrors with silvered glass ones. All that had to be done was to cast a piece of glass to the right size, then plate it with silver. It was this process, which gives excellent results, which was used in making the objective.

The objective was then installed in accordance with Herschel's method. In the Slough astronomer's big telescope, the image of the object, reflected by the inclined mirror at one end of the tube, was formed at the other end, where the ocular was situated. Thus the observer, instead of being placed at the lower end of the tube, hoisted himself up to its upper end, and there, with his magnifying glass, he looked into the huge cylinder. This method had the advantage of eliminating the little mirror whose purpose was to reflect the image to the ocular, so that the image was reflected only once instead of twice. As a result fewer light rays were absorbed, the image was less weakened, and greater brightness was obtained, a valuable advantage in the task of observing the projectile.[1]

Once these decisions had been made, the work was begun. According to the Cambridge Observatory's calculations, the new telescope would have to be 280 feet long, and its mirror would have to be sixteen feet across. Colossal though such an instrument might be, it would not be comparable to the 10,000-foot telescope which the astronomer Hooke proposed building a few years ago. Nevertheless the installation of such a telescope presented great difficulties.

As for the question of location, that was quickly settled. A high mountain had to be chosen, and there are not many high mountains in the United States.

[1] These reflectors are called 'front view telescopes'.

The mountains of that great country consist in fact of two ranges of medium height. Between them flows the magnificent Mississippi, which the Americans would call 'the king of rivers' if they were willing to accept any sort of monarchy.

In the east are the Appalachians, whose tallest peak, in New Hampshire, is 5,600 feet high, which is quite a modest height.

In the west, on the other hand, are the Rocky Mountains, a vast range which begins at the Straits of Magellan, follows the west coast of South America under the name of the Andes, crosses the Isthmus of Panama and stretches across North America all the way to the Arctic.

These mountains are not very high; the Alps or the Himalayas would look down on them with utter disdain from their lofty heights. Their tallest peak is only 10,771 feet high, whereas Mont Blanc is 14,439 feet high, and Kinchinjunga, the highest of the Himalayas, rises 26,776 feet above sea level.

But since the members of the Gun Club wanted the telescope as well as the Columbiad to be within the frontiers of the United States, they had to content themselves with the Rocky Mountains, and all the necessary equipment was sent to Long's Peak, in Missouri.

The difficulties of all sorts which the American engineers had to overcome, and the wonders of daring and skill which they accomplished, could not possibly be described by tongue or pen. It was a real *tour de force*. Immense stones, heavy forged parts, massive corner-irons, the enormous pieces of the cylinder and the objective itself, which alone weighed nearly 30,000 pounds, had to be taken above the snow line, over 10,000 feet high, after being transported across deserted prairies, dense forests and terrifying rapids, far from all centres of population, in wild regions where each detail of life became an almost insoluble problem. Nevertheless the Americans' genius triumphed over these countless obstacles. In the last days of September, less than a year after work had begun, the gigantic tube of the telescope, 240 feet long, hung in the air. It was suspended from an enormous iron framework; an ingenious mechanism enabled the observer to direct it at any point in the sky and follow the heavenly bodies from one horizon to the other as they moved across space.

It had cost over 400,000 dollars. The first time it was aimed at the moon, the observers were seized by an emotion which was half curiosity and half apprehension. What were they going to discover in the field of that 48,000-power telescope? Populations, herds of lunar animals, cities, lakes, oceans? No, they saw nothing that science did not know already, although on every visible part of the moon's disk they were able to determine its volcanic nature with absolute precision.

Before serving the Gun Club, the telescope in the Rocky Mountains rendered immense services to astronomy. Thanks to its great power, it was able to scan the farthest reaches of the heavens; the apparent diameters of a great many stars were rigorously measured, and Mr Clarke of the Cambridge Observatory broke up the crab nebula in Taurus, which Lord Rosse's telescope had never been able to reduce to its component parts.

25

Final details

IT WAS 22nd November. The great departure was to take place ten days later. Only one operation remained to be carried out, a delicate, dangerous operation which required infinite precautions, and against whose success Captain Nicholl had made his third bet: the operation of loading the Columbiad, of putting the 400,000 pounds of gun-cotton into it. Nicholl had thought, not without reason perhaps, that the handling of such an awe-inspiring quantity of gun-cotton would result in a catastrophe, or at any rate that the highly explosive mass would ignite itself under the pressure of the projectile.

The serious dangers involved were increased still further by the nonchalance and frivolity of the Americans who, during the Civil War, did not hesitate to load their bombshells with cigars in their mouths. But Barbicane was determined that his experiment should not fail at the last moment; he therefore chose his best workers, watched them at their work, never taking his eyes off them and, by dint of prudent precautions, was able to put the chances of success in his favour.

First of all, he was careful not to bring the whole charge into the Stone Hill enclosure at once. He had brought it in little by little in sealed wagons. The 400,000 pounds of gun-cotton had been divided into 500-pound portions and placed in 800 bulky cartridge bags made with great care by the best craftsmen in Pensacola. The wagons held ten bags each. They came in one by one on the railway from Tampa. In this way there was never more than 5,000 pounds of gun-cotton within the enclosure at any given time. As soon as each wagon arrived, it was unloaded by barefoot workers and each cartridge bag was taken to the Columbiad and lowered into it by means of hand cranes. All steam machinery had been removed from the vicinity, and even the smallest fires had been put out for two miles around. Merely protecting these masses of gun-cotton from the heat of the sun, even in November, was a major undertaking. The work was therefore done at night whenever possible, with the aid of a Ruhmkorff apparatus which cast a bright artificial light all the way to the bottom of the Columbiad. There the cartridge bags were stacked with perfect regularity and linked by wires which were to carry an electric spark to the centre of each one of them simultaneously.

It was in fact by means of a battery that this mass of gun-cotton was going to be ignited. All the wires, surrounded by an insulating material, were united into a single cable near a narrow opening at the height at which the projectile was to be placed; there it passed through the thick cast-iron wall and went up to the surface through a hole in the stone revetment which had been made for that purpose. When it reached the top of Stone Hill the cable continued for a distance of two miles, supported by poles, until it reached a powerful Bunsen battery, after passing through a switch. It would therefore only be necessary to push the button of the switch to make the current flow instantaneously and ignite the 400,000 pounds of gun-cotton. Needless to say, the battery was not to be activated until the last moment.

By 28th November the 800 cartridge bags were stacked at the bottom of the Columbiad. This part of the operation had been successful. But what worries, anxieties and struggles President Barbicane had been through! He had vainly tried to keep visitors away from Stone Hill; every day people had climbed over the stockade, and some of them had carried rashness to the point of madness by smoking in the midst of the bags of gun-cotton. Barbicane had flown into a rage every day. J. T. Maston had helped as best he could, driving away intruders with great vigour and picking up the burning cigar butts they had tossed here and there. It was a difficult task, for there were more than 300,000 people crowded around the enclosure. Michel Ardan had volunteered to escort the wagons to the mouth of the Columbiad, but when the president of the Gun Club saw him holding a big cigar between his lips as he chased away careless bystanders to whom he was setting a bad example, he realized that he could not count on that daring smoker, and he had to have a special watch set on him in particular.

Finally, since there is a god who looks after artillerymen, nothing blew up and the loading operation was completed. Captain Nicholl was in serious danger of losing his third bet, although the projectile had still to be placed in the Columbiad and lowered onto the thick layer of gun-cotton.

But before beginning that operation, the objects necessary for the journey were methodically stowed in the projectile. There were quite a few of them, and if Michel Ardan had been allowed to have his way they would soon have taken up all the space reserved for the passengers. It was quite incredible how many things that charming Frenchman wanted to take to the moon: a whole cargo of useless trifles. But Barbicane intervened and the list of objects was reduced to what was strictly necessary.

Several thermometers, barometers and telescopes were placed in the instrument chest.

The passengers were eager to examine the moon during the journey; and to facilitate their scrutiny of that new world they decided to take with them Beer and Mädler's excellent map, the *Mappa Selenographica*, printed in four plates and rightly regarded as a masterpiece of observation and patience. It reproduced with scrupulous accuracy the smallest details of that portion of the moon which is turned towards the earth; mountains, valleys, basins, craters, peaks and rilles were shown with their exact dimensions, correct locations and proper names, from Mount Doerfel and Mount Leibnitz, whose tall peak stands in the eastern part of the visible disk, to the *Mare frigoris*, which lies in the northern circumpolar region. It was a valuable document for the travellers, because they could study the new land before they ever set foot on it.

They also took three shotguns and three repeating rifles which fired explosive bullets, plus a very large quantity of powder and shot.

'We don't know whom we may run into,' said Michel Ardan. 'There may be men or animals who won't take kindly to our coming to pay them a visit. So we must take precautions.'

These defensive weapons were accompanied by picks, mattocks, handsaws and other indispensable tools, not to mention clothes suitable for all temperatures, from the cold of the polar regions to the heat of the torrid zone.

Michel Ardan would have liked to take along on his expedition a certain number of animals, though not a couple of every species, for he saw no need to stock the moon with snakes, tigers, alligators and other harmful beasts.

'No,' he said to Barbicane, 'but a few beasts of burden, such as oxen, cows, donkeys or horses, would look good in the landscape and be very useful to us.'

'I agree, my dear Ardan,' replied the president of the Gun Club, 'but our projectile isn't Noah's Ark; it has neither the same capacity nor the same destination. So let's stay within the limits of the possible.'

Finally, after long discussions, it was agreed that the travellers would content themselves with taking along an excellent hunting bitch belonging to Nicholl and a prodigiously strong Newfoundland dog. Several boxes of useful seeds were counted among the essential objects. If Michel Ardan had had his way, he would also have taken a few bags of soil to sow them in. He did in fact take a dozen shrubs which were carefully wrapped in a straw covering and placed in a corner of the projectile.

There remained the important question of food, for they had to take into account the possibility that they would land on an absolutely barren portion of the moon. Barbicane managed to pack a year's supply. This is not surprising when one considers that this food consisted of canned meat and vegetables reduced to their minimum volume by a hydraulic press, and that they

Inside the Columbiad

contained a large amount of nutritive elements. There was not much variety in them, but one could not be particular on such an expedition. There were also fifty gallons of brandy, and a stock of water, though only enough for two months, for as a result of the astronomers' latest observations, no one had any doubt that there was a certain amount of water on the moon. As for food, it would have been ridiculous to believe that inhabitants of the earth would not find anything to eat up there. Michel Ardan did not have the slightest doubt of the subject. If he had had any doubt, he would not have decided to make the journey.

'Besides,' he said one day to his friends, 'we won't be completely abandoned by our comrades on earth, and they'll take care not to forget us.'

'Certainly not!' said J. T. Maston.

'What do you mean?' asked Nicholl.

'It's quite simple,' replied Ardan. 'The Columbiad will still be here, won't it? Well, each time the moon is in a favourable position as regards zenith, if not perigee, which will be about once a year, can't our friends send us a shell full of food, which we'll expect on a certain day?'

'Hurrah!' cried J. T. Maston in the tone of a man who had just hit on an idea of his own. 'Well said! No, my good friends, we won't forget you!'

'I'm sure you won't. So, you see, we'll have regular news from the earth, and we for our part will be terribly inept if we don't find some way of communicating with our good friends down here!'

These words were spoken with such confidence that Michel Ardan, with his air of determination and his superb self-assurance, could have persuaded the whole Gun Club to come with him. What he said seemed simple, elementary, easy and sure to succeed, and a man would have had to have a truly sordid attachment to this wretched terrestrial globe not to accompany the three travellers on their lunar expedition.

When the various objects had been stowed in the projectile, the water intended to act as a shock absorber was poured

M

between the partitions and the gas for lighting purposes was compressed into its container. As for the potassium chlorate and the caustic potash, Barbicane, fearing unexpected delays on the way, took enough to replenish the oxygen and absorb the carbonic acid for two months. An extremely ingenious automatic apparatus was installed to purify the air completely and restore its life-giving properties. The projectile was now ready, and all that remained to be done was to lower it into the Columbiad—though this was going to be an operation filled with difficulties and perils.

The enormous shell was brought to the top of Stone Hill, where powerful cranes seized it and held it suspended above the metal pit-shaft.

This was a tense moment. If the chains had broken under the immense weight, the fall of such a mass would undoubtedly have made the gun-cotton explode.

Fortunately this did not happen, and a few hours later the projectile coach, having been slowly lowered down the bore of the cannon, was resting on its explosive eiderdown of gun-cotton. Its weight had no other effect than to compress the charge of the Columbiad more tightly.

'I've lost,' said the captain, handing President Barbicane three thousand dollars.

Barbicane did not want to take this money from his travelling companion, but he had to yield to Nicholl's insistence; the captain wanted to fulfil all his obligations before leaving the earth.

'Then I can only wish you one thing, Captain,' said Michel Ardan.

'What's that?' asked Nicholl.

'That you'll lose your other two bets! If you do, we'll be sure of getting to the moon!'

26

Fire!

THE first day of December had arrived. It was a fateful day, for if the projectile was not fired that evening at forty-six minutes and forty seconds past ten, more than eighteen years would go by before the moon was in the same simultaneous conditions of zenith and perigee.

The weather was magnificent. In spite of the approach of winter, the sun was shining brightly and bathing in its radiance that globe which was about to lose three of its inhabitants to another world.

How many people slept badly during the night which preceded this impatiently desired day! How many breasts were oppressed by the heavy burden of waiting! All hearts were palpitating with anxiety, except Michel Ardan's. That imperturbable individual came and went with his accustomed air of bustle, but without showing any sign of unusual concern. He had slept peacefully, like Turenne sleeping on a gun carriage before a battle.

Since dawn a vast crowd had covered the plains which extended around Stone Hill as far as the eye could see. Every quarter of an hour the railway from Tampa brought along more sightseers. This immigration soon assumed fantastic proportions, and according to the *Tampa Observer*, five million people trod the soil of Florida on that memorable day.

For a month the greater part of that crowd had been camping around the enclosure and laying the foundations of a town which has since come to be known as Ardansville. The plain was bristling with huts, cabins and shanties, and these ephemeral dwellings housed a population large enough to arouse the envy of the biggest cities in Europe.

Every nation on earth was represented there; all the lan-

The various classes of American society mingled in absolute equality

guages in the world were spoken at once, in a medley of tongues which recalled the biblical times of the Tower of Babel. The various classes of American society mingled in absolute equality. Bankers, farmers, sailors, buyers, brokers, cotton planters, merchants, boatmen and magistrates rubbed elbows with primitive unceremoniousness. Louisiana creoles fraternized with Indiana farmers, gentlemen from Kentucky or Tennessee and elegant, haughty Virginians chatted with half-wild trappers from the Great Lakes and cattle merchants from Cincinnati. Wearing broad-brimmed white beaver hats or traditional Panamas, trousers made of blue cotton from the factories at Opelousas, elegant unbleached linen jackets and brightly coloured boots, they exhibited flamboyant batiste jabots, and on their shirts, cuffs, ties and fingers, and even in their ears glittered a wide assortment of rings, pins, diamonds, chains, ear-rings and trinkets whose costliness was equalled only by their bad taste. Women, children and servants, dressed with equal opulence, accompanied, followed, preceded and surrounded these husbands, fathers and masters who were like tribal chieftains in the midst of their enormous families.

At meal times it was an impressive sight when all these people rushed to the table and, with an appetite which threatened the food supplies of Florida, devoured those dishes peculiar to the southern states which would have been repugnant to a European stomach, such as fricasseed frogs, braised monkey, fish chowder, roast opossum and grilled racoon.

And what a variety of liquors and other drinks came to the aid of that indigestible food! What exciting cries and inviting shouts rang out in bar-rooms or taverns adorned with glasses, mugs, flasks, decanters, incredibly shaped bottles, mortars for pounding sugar and bundles of straw!

'Here's your mint julep!' one of the bartenders would shout.

'Here's you claret sangaree!' another would yelp.

'A gin sling!'

'A brandy smash!'

'Who wants to taste a real mint julep, made in the latest style?' these adroit vendors would call out, tossing the ingredients of that refreshing drink—sugar, lemon, mint, crushed ice, water, brandy and fresh pineapple—from one glass to another with the deftness of a conjuror.

These invitations to throats made thirsty by hot spices were usually repeated simultaneously, producing a deafening din. But on this first day of December such shouts were rare. The bartenders could have shouted themselves hoarse without attracting any customers. Nobody gave a thought to eating or drinking, and at four o'clock there were many people in the crowd who had not yet had their lunch. There was an even more significant symptom: the Americans' violent passion for gambling had been overcome by their excitement. The sight of tenpins lying on their sides, dice sleeping in their cups, motionless roulette wheels, abandoned cribbage boards, and cards used for playing whist, *vingt-et-un*, blackjack, mónte and faro quietly enclosed in their unopened boxes, showed clearly that the great event of the day overshadowed everything else and left no room for diversions.

Until the evening a quiet agitation, of the sort which precedes great catastrophes, ran through that anxious crowd. Every mind was in the grip of an ineffable uneasiness, a painful torpor, an indefinable feeling which clutched the heart. Everybody wished it were already over.

However, at about seven o'clock, this heavy silence was suddenly dissipated. The moon rose above the horizon. Several million hurrahs greeted its appearance. It had kept its appointment. Cheers rose up to the heavens and applause broke out on all sides while fair Phoebe shone peacefully in a beautiful sky and caressed that intoxicated crowd with her most affectionate beams.

Just then the three intrepid travellers appeared, and the cheering grew even louder. Unanimously, instantaneously, the American national anthem burst from every panting breast; and *Yankee Doodle*, sung by a chorus of five million voices, rose like a tempest of sound to the uppermost bounds of the atmosphere.

Then, after that irresistible surge of feeling, the anthem died away, the last voices gradually fell silent, the noises faded and a quiet murmur floated above the deeply moved crowd. Meanwhile the Frenchman and the two Americans had entered the enclosure around which the crowd was pressing. They were accompanied by the members of the Gun Club and the delegation from the European observatories. Barbicane, cool and calm, quietly gave his final orders. Nicholl, his lips pressed tightly together and his hands behind his back, walked with firm, measured steps. Michel Ardan, as nonchalant as ever, dressed like a typical traveller, with leather gaiters on his feet, a game-bag slung over his shoulder, his brown velvet clothes hanging loosely from his body and a cigar between his teeth, was distributing warm handshakes with princely prodigality as he walked along. His gaiety and verve were irrepressible; he laughed, joked and played childish tricks on the dignified J. T. Maston; in short, he was French and, even worse, Parisian to the very end.

Ten o'clock struck. The time had come for the travellers to take their places in the projectile. It would take a certain amount of time to lower them into it, screw down the door-plates, and remove the cranes and scaffolding from the mouth of the Columbiad.

The engineer Murchison, who was going to ignite the gun-cotton by means of an electric spark, had synchronized his chronometer to within a tenth of a second of Barbicane's. The travellers enclosed in the projectile would thus be able to watch the impassive moving hand which would mark the instant of their departure.

The time for farewells had come. It was a touching scene. In spite of his feverish gaiety, Michel Ardan felt moved. J. T. Maston had found under his dry lids an old tear which he had probably been keeping for this occasion. He shed it on the forehead of his dear and worthy president.

'Why don't I come with you?' he said. 'There's still time!'

'Impossible, old fellow,' replied Barbicane.

A few moments later, the three travellers had installed themselves in the projectile and screwed down the door-plate. The mouth of the Columbiad, cleared of all obstructions, was open to the sky.

Who could ever describe the universal excitement which had now reached its peak?

The moon was moving across a limpid sky, extinguishing the glittering stars on its way. It was now crossing the Gemini constellation and was nearly half way between the horizon and the zenith. It was easy for everyone to understand that the projectile was going to be aimed ahead of its target, as the hunter aims in front of the hare he wants to hit.

A terrifying silence hung over the whole scene. There was not a breath of wind on the earth; not a breath of air in any breast. Hearts no longer dared to beat. The crowd's fearful eyes were fixed on the gaping mouth of the Columbiad.

Murchison was watching the hand of his chronometer. There were barely forty seconds before the moment of departure, and each one of them was like a century.

At the twentieth second a quiver ran through the crowd as it occurred to everybody that the daring travellers inside the projectile were also counting the terrible seconds. Isolated cries broke out:

'Thirty-five! . . . Thirty-six! . . . Thirty-seven! . . . Thirty-eight! . . . Thirty-nine! . . . Forty! Fire!!!'

Murchison pressed the switch, restoring the current and sending an electric spark into the depths of the Columbiad.

Instantly there was a terrifying, fantastic, superhuman explosion which could not be compared to any known sound, not even a clap of thunder or the roar of an eruption. An immense jet of flame shot from the bowels of the earth as from a crater. The ground heaved, and only a few people caught a brief glimpse of the projectile victoriously cleaving the air in the midst of clouds of blazing vapour.

27

Cloudy weather

As THE incandescent jet rose into the sky to a prodigious height, the blossoming flames lit up the whole of Florida, and for an incalculable instant day was substituted for night over a considerable stretch of country. The huge plume of fire was seen from a hundred miles at sea, in the Atlantic as well as in the Gulf of Mexico, and more than one ship's captain recorded the appearance of a gigantic meteor in his log.

The firing of the Columbiad was accompanied by a positive earthquake. Florida was shaken to its very entrails. The gases released by the gun-cotton, expanded by heat, pushed back the layers of the atmosphere with incomparable violence, and this artificial hurricane, a hundred times swifter than any natural tempest, passed through the air like a whirlwind.

Not one spectator had remained standing: men, women and children were all flattened like wheat before a storm. There was an indescribable tumult and a great many people were seriously injured. J. T. Maston, who, against all prudence, had taken up a position too far forward, was thrown back a hundred feet and passed like a cannon-ball over his fellow citizens' heads. Three hundred thousand people were temporarily deafened and stupefied.

The violent wind blew down huts, knocked over cabins, uprooted trees within a radius of twenty miles, drove trains all the way back to Tampa, and struck the town itself like an avalanche, destroying over a hundred buildings, including

Saint Mary's Church and the new stock exchange building, which was cracked from one end to the other. Some of the boats in the harbour were thrown against each other and sank, while a dozen ships in the roadstead were tossed up on shore after snapping their anchor chains as if they were threads. But the area of devastation extended even farther, beyond the frontiers of the United States. The effect of the blast, aided by the west wind, was felt far out in the Atlantic, over three hundred miles from the American coast. An artificial storm, which Admiral FitzRoy had been unable to foresee, struck ships at sea with incredible violence. Several vessels were caught in these frightful cyclones before they had time to lower their sails, and sank under full canvas; they included the *Childe Harold* from Liverpool, and this became the subject of fierce recriminations on the part of England.

Finally, to leave no incident unrecorded, although the report is guaranteed by nothing more than the affirmations of a few natives, half an hour after the departure of the projectile a number of people in Gorea and Sierra Leone claimed to have heard a muffled boom, the last remnant of sound waves which had crossed the Atlantic and come to die on the African coast.

But we must return to Florida. When the first moment of panic had passed, the whole crowd, including even the injured and the deafened, collected its wits, and frenzied shouts of 'Hurrah for Ardan! Hurrah for Barbicane! Hurrah for Nicholl!' rose up to the skies. Several million people, forgetting their bruises and consternation and thinking only of the projectile, looked up into space through telescopes, field-glasses and binoculars. But they looked in vain: the projectile had disappeared from sight. They had to resign themselves to waiting for telegrams from Long's Peak. Mr Belfast, the director of the Cambridge Observatory, and a skilled and persevering astronomer, had been given the task of observing the projectile, and he was at his post in the Rocky Mountains.

But an unforeseen, though easily foreseeable phenomenon, about which nothing could be done, soon put the public's patience to a severe test.

The clear weather suddenly changed : the sky darkened as it was covered with clouds. How could it have been otherwise, after the terrible displacement of the atmospheric layers, and the dispersion of the enormous quantity of vapour produced by the explosion of 400,000 pounds of gun-cotton? The whole natural order had been disturbed. There is nothing surprising about this, since it has often been observed that atmospheric conditions can be abruptly modified by the firing of big guns in a naval battle.

The next day the sun rose above a horizon laden with thick clouds, a heavy, impenetrable curtain between heaven and earth which unfortunately extended as far as the Rocky Mountains. It was a disaster. A chorus of protests arose all over the globe. But Nature took no notice of it ; since men had disturbed the atmosphere with their explosion, they would clearly have to take the consequences.

During this first day, everyone tried to see through the veil of thick clouds, but to no avail. In any case, everyone was mistaken in looking up, for as a result of the earth's rotation the projectile was now moving away from the antipodes.

Be that as it may, when deep, impenetrable darkness enveloped the earth and the moon rose once more above the horizon, it could not be seen ; it seemed to be deliberately hiding from the audacious men who had fired at it. No observations were possible, and telegrams from Long's Peak confirmed this regrettable *contretemps*.

However, if the experiment was successful, the travellers, who had set off at forty-six minutes and forty seconds past ten on the evening of 1st December, would arrive on 4th December at midnight. The world resigned itself to waiting till then, especially as it would have been quite difficult to observe an object as small as the projectile in these conditions.

On 4th December, between eight o'clock and midnight, it should have been possible to follow the path of the projectile, which would have appeared as a black dot on the bright surface of the moon. But the weather remained mercilessly cloudy. The public's exasperation knew no bounds. Some people went so far as to shout insults at the moon for not showing itself—a sad turn of events.

J. T. Maston set off for Long's Peak in despair. He wanted to see for himself. He had no doubt that his friends had reached their destination. There had been no reports that the projectile had fallen on any of the earth's islands and continents, and J. T. Maston refused to admit the possibility that it might have fallen into one of the oceans which cover three-quarters of the globe's surface.

On 5th December the weather was unchanged. The great telescopes of the Old World, those of Herschel, Rosse and Foucault, were kept constantly aimed at the moon, for the weather was magnificent in Europe, but the relative weakness of those instruments made any useful observation impossible.

On 6th December the sky seemed to change a little. There was hope, but it did not last long, and by the evening the thick clouds were again defending the starry firmament against all eyes.

The matter was now becoming serious, for on 11th December at eleven minutes past nine in the morning, the moon was due to enter its last quarter. After that it would start waning, and even if the sky should clear, the chances of observation would be greatly lessened, for the moon would henceforth show a constantly decreasing portion of its surface, and would finally become new : in other words, it would rise and set with the sun, whose rays would make it absolutely invisible. It would not be full again until 3rd January, at forty-seven minutes past twelve, and observations could not begin until then.

The newspapers published these facts with long commentaries, and did not conceal from the public that it would have to show angelic patience.

On 8th December, nothing. On the ninth the sun appeared for a moment, as if to taunt the Americans. It was greeted with jeers, and, doubtless offended by this reception, it showed itself extremely stingy with its rays.

On the tenth, there was no change. J. T. Maston nearly went mad, and there were fears for the worthy man's brain, which had hitherto been so well preserved beneath his gutta-percha cranium.

But on the eleventh one of those appalling storms which occur in semi-tropical regions arose. Strong east winds swept away the clouds which had been piled up for so long, and that evening the half-consumed disk of the Queen of the Night passed majestically among the limpid constellations of the sky.

28

A new star

THAT very night, the exciting news which had been so impatiently awaited burst like a bombshell over every state in the Union, then raced across the ocean and sped along every telegraph wire in the world. The projectile had been sighted, thanks to the gigantic telescope on Long's Peak.

Here is the report drawn up by the Director of the Cambridge Observatory. It contains the scientific conclusion of the Gun Club's great experiment:

Long's Peak, 12 December

To the Staff of the Cambridge Observatory

The projectile launched by the Columbiad at Stone Hill was sighted by J. Belfast and J. T. Maston on 12th December, at 8.47 p.m. with the moon in its last quarter.

The projectile has not reached its goal. It has passed to one side of it, but close enough to be caught by the moon's gravity.

Its rectilinear motion has changed to an extremely rapid circular motion, and it has now become a satellite of the moon, moving in an elliptical orbit around it.

It has not yet been possible to determine the characteristics of this new star: neither its speed of revolution nor its speed of rotation is known. Its distance from the surface of the moon may be estimated at approximately 2,833 miles.

There are now two possibilities: either the moon's gravity

will prevail, and the travellers will reach their destination, or the projectile will be held in an immutable orbit and will continue to move around the moon until the end of time.

Observation will one day tell us which of these hypotheses is correct, but so far the only results of the Gun Club's project has been to add a new heavenly body to our solar system.

J. BELFAST

What a host of questions this unexpected outcome raised! What mysteries lay in store for scientific investigation! Thanks to the courage and devotion of three men, this apparently frivolous enterprise of sending a projectile to the moon had just produced an amazing result whose consequences were incalculable. Although the travellers, imprisoned in their new satellite, had not reached their goal, they were at least part of the lunar system: they were circling the Queen of the Night, and for the first time human eyes were able to penetrate all its mysteries. The names of Nicholl, Barbicane and Michel Ardan would forever be famous in the annals of astronomy, for these bold explorers, eager to extend the limits of human knowledge, had fearlessly flung themselves into space and risked their lives in the strangest undertaking of modern times.

Be that as it may, when the Long's Peak report became known, there was a feeling of surprise and fear all over the world. Was it possible to go to the aid of those brave inhabitants of the earth? No, it seemed, for they had placed themselves outside mankind by going beyond the limits which God had imposed on earthly creatures. They had enough air for two months and enough food for a year. But after that? Even the most insensitive hearts palpitated at this terrible question.

One man alone refused to admit that the situation was hopeless; one man alone still had confidence. That man was the explorers' devoted friend, as bold and resolute as they were: the worthy J. T. Maston.

He was keeping his eye on them. His residence was now the Long's Peak station, his horizon the mirror of the huge reflector. As soon as the moon rose each night, he framed it in the field of the telescope, never losing sight of it for a moment and assiduously following its movement through space. With unremitting patience he watched the projectile pass across its silvery disk, and thus the worthy man remained in constant communion with his three friends, whom he still hoped to see again one day.

'We'll communicate with them,' he said to anyone who would listen, 'as soon as circumstances permit. We'll hear from them and they'll hear from us! I know them: they're ingenious men. Among the three of them they've taken into space all the resources of art, science and industry. With that you can do anything you want, and they'll find a way out of their trouble, just you wait and see!'

Titles in this Series of Illustrated Classics

CHILDREN'S ILLUSTRATED CLASSICS

(Illustrated Classics for Older Readers are listed on fourth page)

Andrew Lang's **ADVENTURES OF ODYSSEUS.** Illustrated by KIDDELL-MONROE.
The wanderings of the great Greek hero on his way home to Ithaca.

AESOP'S FABLES. Illustrated by KIDDELL-MONROE.
A definitive translation by John Warrington.

Lewis Carroll's **ALICE'S ADVENTURES IN WONDERLAND and THROUGH THE LOOKING-GLASS.** Illustrated by JOHN TENNIEL.

George MacDonald's **AT THE BACK OF THE NORTH WIND.** Illustrated by E. H. SHEPARD.
This is the lovable and much loved story of Diamond.

Robert Louis Stevenson's **THE BLACK ARROW.** Illustrated by LIONEL EDWARDS.
The period is the England of the Wars of the Roses.

Anna Sewell's **BLACK BEAUTY.** Illustrated by LUCY KEMP-WELCH.

Roger Lancelyn Green's **A BOOK OF MYTHS.** Illustrated by KIDDELL-MONROE.
A retelling of the world's greatest legends and folk-tales.

THE BOOK OF NONSENSE. Edited by ROGER LANCELYN GREEN. Illustrated by CHARLES FOLKARD in colour, and with original drawings by TENNIEL, LEAR, FURNISS, HOLIDAY, HUGHES, SHEPARD and others.
Examples of 'nonsense' from ancient to modern times.

THE BOOK OF VERSE FOR CHILDREN. Collected by ROGER LANCELYN GREEN. Illustrated with two-colour drawings in the text by MARY SHILLABEER. (Not available in the U.S.A. in this edition.)

Mrs Ewing's **THE BROWNIES AND OTHER STORIES.** Illustrated by E. H. SHEPARD.

Mrs Molesworth's **THE CARVED LIONS.** Illustrated by LEWIS HART.
An evocative story of the Manchester of a century ago.

Captain Marryat's **THE CHILDREN OF THE NEW FOREST.** Illustrated by LIONEL EDWARDS.
A story of adventure in a wild and romantic corner of England.

Robert Louis Stevenson's **A CHILD'S GARDEN OF VERSES.** Illustrated by MARY SHILLABEER.
This collection contains a number of poems not found in other editions.

Charles Dickens's **A CHRISTMAS CAROL and THE CRICKET ON THE HEARTH.** Illustrated by C. E. BROCK.

R. M. Ballantyne's **THE CORAL ISLAND.** Illustrated by LEO BATES.
Ballantyne's most famous boys' book is illustrated with such realism that the most fascinating of islands in boys' fiction is more vivid than ever.

Susan Coolidge's **WHAT KATY DID.** Illustrated by MARGERY GILL.

Mrs Molesworth's THE CUCKOO CLOCK. Illustrated by E. H. SHEPARD.
Shepard's exquisite and delicate drawings enhance the enthralling text.

E. Nesbit's THE ENCHANTED CASTLE. Illustrated by CECIL LESLIE.
A sunny garden leads to a never-never land of enchantment.

FAIRY TALES FROM THE ARABIAN NIGHTS. Illustrated by KIDDELL-MONROE.
Here are the favourite tales—the fairy tales—out of the many told in the 'Thousand and One Nights'.

FAIRY TALES OF LONG AGO. Edited by M. C. CAREY. Illustrated by D. J. WATKINS-PITCHFORD.
This varied collection takes in translations from Charles Perrault, Madame de Beaumont, the Countess d'Aulnoy of France, Asbjörnsen and Moe, etc.

Selma Lagerlöf's THE FURTHER ADVENTURES OF NILS. Illustrated by HANS BAUMHAUER.
Nils's adventures continue with his flight over lake, hill, ice, snow, forest and moor of Sweden. The artist ably interprets the visual contrasts of the journey. (Not available in the U.S.A. in this edition.) *See also* THE WONDERFUL ADVENTURES OF NILS (on third page).

Louisa M. Alcott's GOOD WIVES. Illustrated by S. VAN ABBÉ.

Frances Browne's GRANNY'S WONDERFUL CHAIR. Illustrated by DENYS WATKINS-PITCHFORD.
The author, blind from birth, draws upon the Irish fairy-stories of her childhood to add magic and colour to the whole of this enchanting book.

GRIMMS' FAIRY TALES. Illustrated by CHARLES FOLKARD.

HANS ANDERSEN'S FAIRY TALES. Illustrated by HANS BAUMHAUER.
A new English rendering, including some new and outstanding tales.

Mary Mapes Dodge's HANS BRINKER. Illustrated by HANS BAUMHAUER.
This story is the best known and best loved work of the author.

Johanna Spyri's HEIDI. Illustrated by VINCENT O. COHEN.
This is the famous story of a Swiss child and her life among the Alps.

Charles Kingsley's THE HEROES. Illustrated by KIDDELL-MONROE.
A retelling of the legends of Perseus, the Argonauts and Theseus.

Louisa M. Alcott's JO'S BOYS. Illustrated by HARRY TOOTHILL.
'There is an abiding charm about the story.' *Scotsman.*

A. M. Hadfield's KING ARTHUR AND THE ROUND TABLE. Illustrated by DONALD SETON CAMMELL.
The haunting world of the Round Table.

Charlotte M. Yonge's THE LITTLE DUKE. Illustrated by MICHAEL GODFREY.
The story of Richard the Fearless, Duke of Normandy from 942 to 996.

Frances Hodgson Burnett's LITTLE LORD FAUNTLEROY.
'The best version of the Cinderella story in a modern idiom that exists.'
MARGHANITA LASKI.

Louisa M. Alcott's LITTLE MEN. Illustrated by HARRY TOOTHILL.
Harry Toothill's drawings capture the liveliness of a young gentlemen's academy.

Louisa M. Alcott's LITTLE WOMEN. Illustrated by S. VAN ABBÉ.
S. van Abbé's drawings capture the vivacity and charm of the March family.

Mrs Ewing's LOB LIE-BY-THE-FIRE and THE STORY OF A SHORT LIFE.
Illustrated by RANDOLPH CALDECOTT ('Lob') and H. M. BROCK ('Short Life').
Two of Mrs Ewing's most charming stories.

MODERN FAIRY STORIES. Edited by ROGER LANCELYN GREEN. Illustrated by E. H. SHEPARD.
Original (not 'retold') fairy stories by thirteen authors of modern times.

Jean Ingelow's MOPSA THE FAIRY. Illustrated by DORA CURTIS.
A river journey leads to the realms of wonder.

NURSERY RHYMES. Collected and illustrated in two-colour line by A. H. WATSON.
A comprehensive book of nursery rhymes.

Carlo Collodi's PINOCCHIO. The Story of a Puppet. Illustrated by CHARLES FOLKARD.
The most enchanting story of a puppet ever written.

Andrew Lang's PRINCE PRIGIO and PRINCE RICARDO. Illustrated by D. J. WATKINS-PITCHFORD.
Two modern fairy tales, rich in romantic adventures.

George MacDonald's THE LOST PRINCESS
THE PRINCESS AND CURDIE
THE PRINCESS AND THE GOBLIN
The first two volumes illustrated by CHARLES FOLKARD, the third by D. J. WATKINS-PITCHFORD.

Carola Oman's ROBIN HOOD. Illustrated by S. VAN ABBÉ.
Carola Oman lends substance to the 'Prince of Outlaws'.

W. M. Thackeray's THE ROSE AND THE RING and Charles Dickens's THE MAGIC FISH-BONE.
Two children's stories, the first containing the author's illustrations, the latter containing PAUL HOGARTH's work.

J. R. Wyss's THE SWISS FAMILY ROBINSON. Illustrated by CHARLES FOLKARD.
This is a new version by Audrey Clark of the popular classic.

Charles and Mary Lamb's TALES FROM SHAKESPEARE. Illustrated by ARTHUR RACKHAM.

TALES OF MAKE-BELIEVE. Edited by ROGER LANCELYN GREEN. Illustrated by HARRY TOOTHILL.
Charles Dickens, Rudyard Kipling, E. Nesbit, Thomas Hardy, E. V. Lucas, etc.

Nathaniel Hawthorne's TANGLEWOOD TALES. Illustrated by S. VAN ABBÉ.
This is a sequel to the famous *Wonder Book*.

Thomas Hughes's TOM BROWN'S SCHOOLDAYS. Illustrated by S. VAN ABBÉ.
'The best story of a boy's schooldays ever written.'

Charles Kingsley's THE WATER-BABIES. Illustrated by ROSALIE K. FRY.
The artist's drawings delicately interpret the fantastic beauty of the underwater world.

Susan Coolidge's WHAT KATY DID. Illustrated by MARGERY GILL.
A heroine who learns to take responsibility and finds happiness in doing so.

Nathaniel Hawthorne's A WONDER BOOK. Illustrated by S. VAN ABBÉ.
Hawthorne's famous *Wonder Book* recalls the immortal fables of antiquity.

Selma Lagerlöf's THE WONDERFUL ADVENTURES OF NILS. Illustrated by HANS BAUMHAUER.
Translated into most languages of the world, this Swedish tale of the boy who rode on the back of a young gander and flew northwards to find surprising adventures is a great favourite. (Not available in the U.S.A. in this edition.)
See also THE FURTHER ADVENTURES OF NILS.

A Selection of
Illustrated Classics for Older Readers

Jules Verne's AROUND THE WORLD IN EIGHTY DAYS. Illustrated by W. F. PHILLIPPS.
The new translation by Robert and Jacqueline Baldick demonstrates here Verne's lively story-telling genius better than ever before.

Jack London's THE CALL OF THE WILD. Illustrated by CHARLES PICKARD.
This story of a dog called Buck is unique for its penetration into the uncanny understanding and reactions of a wild creature to moments of extreme tension.

Jean Webster's DADDY-LONG-LEGS. Illustrated by HARRY FAIRBAIRN.

Cervantes's DON QUIXOTE. Illustrated by W. HEATH ROBINSON.
An edition suitably edited from the Cervantes original.

Jonathan Swift's GULLIVER'S TRAVELS. Illustrated by ARTHUR RACKHAM.
Gulliver's Travels is one of the great satires in the English language.

Oscar Wilde's THE HAPPY PRINCE AND OTHER STORIES. Illustrated by PEGGY FORTNUM.

Edith Nesbit's THE HOUSE OF ARDEN. Illustrated by CLARKE HUTTON.
Magic and reality have little dividing line in this story where the Arden children, in search of the family treasure to repair the fortunes of the Arden estate, find themselves spirited away in a moment to Tudor days, the Napoleonic wars and Cromwell's Commonwealth.

Mark Twain's THE PRINCE AND THE PAUPER. Illustrated by ROBERT HODGSON.
The tale of a London beggar boy who changed places with the young prince of the realm—and found it difficult to cope with matters of state.

Anthony Hope's THE PRISONER OF ZENDA. Illustrated by MICHAEL GODFREY.
The Ruritanian romance in which Rudolph Rassendyll saves the Elphbergs' throne.

Erskine Childers's THE RIDDLE OF THE SANDS. Illustrated by CHARLES MOZLEY.
A thrilling adventure story on the North Frisian coast before World War I.

Daniel Defoe's ROBINSON CRUSOE. Illustrated by J. AYTON SYMINGTON.

Anthony Hope's RUPERT OF HENTZAU. Illustrated by MICHAEL GODFREY.
The enthralling sequel to *The Prisoner of Zenda.*

TEN TALES OF DETECTION. Edited by ROGER LANCELYN GREEN. Illustrated by IAN RIBBONS.
Conan Doyle's Sherlock Holmes and other famous detectives of fiction.

Mark Twain's TOM SAWYER
HUCKLEBERRY FINN
These two Twain classics are superbly illustrated by C. WALTER HODGES.

Roger Lancelyn Green's THE TALE OF ANCIENT ISRAEL. Illustrated by CHARLES KEEPING.

THIRTEEN UNCANNY TALES. Illustrated by RAY OGDEN.
F. Anstey, M. R. James, Sir Arthur Conan Doyle, H. G. Wells and others.

Ernest Thompson Seton's THE TRAIL OF THE SANDHILL STAG and Other Lives of the Hunted. Illustrated with drawings by the author and coloured frontispiece by RITA PARSONS.

Robert Louis Stevenson's TREASURE ISLAND. Illustrated by S. VAN ABBÉ.
Probably no other illustrator of this famous tale has portrayed so vividly the characters in a book that lives so long in a boy's imagination.

Jack London's WHITE FANG. Illustrated by CHARLES PICKARD.
The famous story of a wild creature, part dog, part wolf; and his treatment under brutal masters and one that showed him affection.

Frank L. Baum's THE WONDERFUL WIZARD OF OZ. Illustrated by B. S. BIRO.
THE MARVELLOUS LAND OF OZ. Illustrated by B. S. BIRO.

Further volumes in preparation